THE EYE OF RA

Book 1

Ben Gartner

Annotation Key

In margin	Underline/Highlight or Use Codes
V	Vocabulary word
R	Text showing reference (historical, cultural, sustainability)
LD	Underline examples of literary devices (<u>M</u>etaphor, <u>S</u>imile, Personification, Imagery, <u>ID</u>iom, <u>A</u>llusion, <u>F</u>oreshadowing)
CD	Character development
?	<u>Text</u> questions you have about the text
!	<u>Text</u> you find interesting and might want to locate again
Notes	<u>Text</u> with signposts
	Bullet point key plot points at the end of each chapter

Praise for *The Eye of Ra* series

⭐ Gold Recipient, *Mom's Choice Awards Honoring Excellence*

⭐ Silver Medal in Children's Adventure, *2020 International Readers' Favorite Awards*

⭐ Award-winning Finalist, *Next Generation Book Awards*

⭐ 1st Place in both Children's Adventure AND Grades 4th-6th, *2020 TopShelf Awards*

⭐ Grand Prize Winner, *Colorado Author Project*

⭐ 1st Place, *Gertrude Warner Middle Grade Fiction Award*

"An engaging, eventful, history-based fantasy with realistic protagonists and an enjoyable, twist-filled plot." —*Kirkus Reviews* on *The Eye of Ra*

"Once again, Gartner deftly weaves real-life history into a compelling adventure, offering high-stakes, realistic danger and vivid scene-setting." —*Kirkus Reviews* on *Sol Invictus*

"Gartner's middle grade time-travel adventure is a rollicking ride . . . this adventure novel hits the sweet spot. " —*BookLife Reviews by Publishers Weekly* on *The Eye of Ra*

"Gartner has a knack for action and creating compelling historical personalities . . . Middle readers who treasure ancient history with a side of adventure will welcome this fantasy story." —*BookLife Reviews by Publishers Weekly* on *Sol Invictus*

"Gartner's narrative voice complements the book's brisk pacing and heightens its unending action…The book echoes the same adventure-driven narrative of Percy Jackson and the Olympians but with its own Roman twist. However,

Gartner skillfully embellishes a narrow glimpse of history that is typically studied for its grander narrative." —*BookLife Prize, 2021* on *Sol Invictus*

"Ben Gartner has a gift for capturing details of the past and weaving a story that brings the adventure out of history. This series creates a love of history and learning with the wonder and excitement that the siblings find when they travel back in time." —*Readers' Favorite*

"Fun, action-packed read, with a healthy dose of historical facts. Kids will be hooked on this one!" —Adam Perry, author of *The Magicians of Elephant County*

"A heartwarming and fun action adventure novel for the whole family. Full of interesting historical tidbits and fun mishaps, *The Eye of Ra* keeps the pages turning. An excellent read! " —Kerelyn Smith, author of *Mulrox and the Malcognitos*

"With tons of action, humor, excellent character development, and historical details that will make you feel like you've been swept back in time too, this is sure to be a winner for middle grade readers." —Sam Subity, author of *The Last Shadow Warrior*

"*The Eye of Ra* is a delightfully quick and smart magical tour of ancient Egypt, giving middle grade readers an educational survey from the perspective of a modern kid without ever feeling like a lecture." —Jason Henderson, author of *Young Captain Nemo*

"This book was awesome! The book captivated me." —10-year-old book blogger from *Fantastic Books and Where to Find Them*

Also By Ben Gartner

Sol Invictus
People of the Sun

Copyright © 2020 Ben Gartner

bengartner.com

Published in the United States of America by Crescent Vista Press. Please direct all inquiries to crescentvistapress.com.

Cover by Anne Glenn Design

Library of Congress Control Number: 2019920427

ISBN: 978-1-7341552-1-1 (paperback)
ISBN: 978-1-7341552-4-2 (hardcover)
ISBN: 978-1-7341552-0-4 (ebook)

First Edition, 2020

To my sons, who invented this story with me.
Your collaboration is priceless.

CHAPTER ONE

Summer Break

JOHN

John Tidewell flashed a sly smirk, revealing the lone dimple in his right cheek amid freckle constellations, as he watched Mr. Maxton at the head of the class. Their teacher wore a long black-haired wig and star-shaped glasses and he swung his arm around and around riffing on the air guitar only he could see, while his mouth twisted in the exaggerated howls of Alice Cooper's famous ode to the end of the year: "School's Out."

Thank goodness the end-of-school bell saved John and his classmates from more of their teacher's terrible serenading. Yep, there it was. The end of fourth grade. The beginning of summer. Is there anything as wonderful as summer?

John's stomach tingled with giddy bubbles as he thought of all the fun that comes with summer vacation: days at the lake, hikes, summer camp, trips with the family, pickup basketball games with his best friend, Roman—

John paused and looked down at his Nike basketball high-tops, a birthday gift from Roman.

"Come on, John!" Roman patted him on the shoulder before dashing over to the posts where the backpacks hung. Roman had a wide nose and deep-set eyes with a low forehead. Though built stocky, unlike the traditional basketball physique, Roman was light on his feet like all the greats and a valuable ally on the court.

But there'd be no basketball games with Roman *this* summer.

The Tidewells—John's family—were moving in a week, away from Colorado and out to Maryland because of a job transfer for John's dad.

John sighed. He hadn't been sleeping much and

he felt tired. But this was more than a regular kind of tired, this was a heavy, walk-slow kind of tired. A *Do I really have to get out of bed?* after ten hours of sleep kind of tired. John didn't know anyone in Maryland. He could barely remember where it was on a map. They didn't have any mountains. And, most important, his best friend, Roman, was here in Colorado. His fort was here, his favorite hikes were here, the bike loop where he'd clocked a record twenty-seven seconds was here. But in Maryland . . .

The rest of his classmates (old classmates, now) brushed past him, excited to get going, some hooting and hollering. Not looking where he was going, John smacked into a girl and dropped his backpack, startled, his hands up in alarm.

"Sorry!" he yelled. She scampered out the door not even noticing him.

Roman put his hand on John's shoulder. "You okay?"

John opened his mouth but didn't know how to answer the question, so he closed his jaw and shrugged, looking down again.

"Wanna shoot some hoops?" Roman asked.

John's lips curled up in a smile. "Always."

SARAH

Sarah Tidewell couldn't wait for the adventurous summer ahead. They were moving to Maryland! Close to Washington, DC, its free museums, the ocean, so many new places to see and people to meet. Walking down the hall of her middle school, she looked around with her head held high and an easy smile on her lips.

"Goodbye, sixth grade!" She'd worn her glittery sequined shirt for the last day of school, so it fit well when she gave her best princess wave with a cup of her hand to the block of stacked steel rectangles lining the hall. "Goodbye, funky green lockers. Goodbye, glass case of trophies. Goodbye, cafeteria. Goodbye—"

"Oh, come off it, Sarah," said the girl on her left, Cynthia. The bright yellow bow in her hair bounced when she laughed.

Sarah flipped her long red hair in a mock dismissal toward her friend.

The girl on her right, Maxine, said, "Yeah, we'll miss you too, Sarah." She rolled her eyes. Maxine wore a button-up collared shirt that made her look like an older boy.

Sarah turned to her and with a curtsy said, "Goodbye, Maxine Johnson, princess of sarcasm." Then she turned to Cynthia. "Goodbye, my dearest and bestest and only true friend, Cynthia Cummings. I'll miss you most of all."

"Oh, get a room, sheesh," Maxine said, slapping Sarah on the back.

All three girls giggled and leaned into one another for a group hug. In the huddle, Sarah dropped the royal routine and added, "Seriously, you have to come out and visit me in Maryland. It's going to be awesome."

"Boys?" Cynthia asked.

"I hear they have some of those on the East Coast too," Sarah said.

"Yeah," Maxine scoffed. "The mysterious types with dark eyes." She pushed up her black-rimmed glasses.

"Are you going to New York?" Cynthia asked, bubbling like a bath bomb, swaying in her dance stretch pants.

"Why not?" Sarah threw her hands into the air and flung her head out of the huddle. "I want to visit everywhere!"

"Everywhere?" Maxine asked. "Even the sandy desert of the Sahara?"

"Everywhere!" Sarah skipped off down the hall, leaving her friends behind. "Why not?"

CHAPTER TWO

A Mysterious Cave

JOHN

"I don't want to go," John whined to his mom and dad as they finished dinner together. John had wolfed down the meal, one of his favorites: herb-roasted chicken, green beans, and red potatoes pan fried in butter. His mom always called him "Little Chef," since, as she said, he seemed to have a "refined palate." John wasn't exactly sure what that meant, but he enjoyed helping his parents in the kitchen, especially when he got to choose what they ate for dinner.

John excused himself from the table and rinsed

his dish, then put it in the dishwasher. "What about Monopoly instead?"

Still hopeful for a last-minute stay of execution from the hike he didn't want to do, John thought one of their favorite pastimes would be a convincing argument.

"This will be our last family hike for a while," Mom said. "In Colorado, at least. Please, John?"

"Let's go!" Sarah bounded to the bench next to the back door and sat, putting on her worn hiking boots.

"Don't forget your water bottle, sweetie," Dad said, holding up a blue steel cylinder. "Always so eager to go, go, go. You're like your mother."

"There's so much to see!" Sarah said, and spun in a circle. She winced and rubbed at the small scar on her right temple. Last year, she'd hit the corner of a picnic table while attempting to jump over it on a skateboard.

"Doesn't mean you shouldn't plan or be careful," John said.

"Ugh," Sarah responded with an emphatic roll of her eyes until John saw only whites in her sockets. "Gotta live a little, John."

"Sarah," Dad said, giving her the "look" that meant she'd said something insensitive. John had heard them have that conversation numerous times.

"What about ice cream first?" John asked.

"Here's your water," Mom said, handing another steel bottle to John. "How about ice cream when we get back from the hike?"

"Fine," John said. "A short one."

"Who knows, you might have fun," Dad said, ruffling John's hair. John swatted the hand away and scowled.

Dad put both palms up. "Okay, okay."

"What're you thinking?" Mom asked Dad.

"Let's do Crescent Vista," Dad said. "Should be a beautiful sunset tonight." He held up a flashlight and dropped it into his own backpack, then handed one to his wife, and Sarah and John too. "Just in case."

"Let's do it!" Sarah yanked open the kitchen door to the backyard and skipped off to the gate in the fence.

"All the way 'til sunset?" John whined, imagining his tired legs already. "I thought you said it'd be a quick one."

"It will," Dad said. "Sunset is only about an hour away. One last view of these beautiful mountains before we leave for the flatland and the sea."

Mom smiled at Dad in a loving way that made John happy, then she leaned in and kissed her husband on the cheek.

John trudged out the back door and looked up the slope of the towering pine trees.

Above the forest, leaning in like a king whispering a secret, the line of mountains arced gracefully against the purple sky of dusk. A lazy cloud stretched out against one pinnacle, reclining, waiting for the sunset show.

As a family, they set off up the mountain on a familiar trail. John knew this hike well. The overlook from Crescent Vista could steal your breath away. Especially after hiking up the steep incline to get there.

The angle of the terrain, mixed with the rocky ledges and the plentiful trees, made for excellent fort-building territory. Going around one switch-back, a bit of nostalgia came over John when he remembered one such hideaway that he and Sarah had built together—before she stopped being interested in forts. Nothing more than a lean-to bare-ly big enough for the both of their bodies, with some pine boughs as a roof. But it had felt cozy, not small.

"Sarah," John said between panting breaths. "Remember Fort Tidewell?" He gestured off to a clump of trees off trail.

Sarah stopped and smiled, chuffing some air from her nose and taking a swig from her water. "Of course. Defend Fort Tidewell from the Sasquatch!"

John laughed. "Oh, yeah! I totally forgot about the attack of the Sasquatch. That was so fun."

"Also known as the weird hairy animal doll Aunt Lorraine made me, whatever that was supposed to be," Sarah said, chuckling.

"Didn't you bury that thing out there?"

Sarah's eyes looked up and to the left as she reminisced, then she started nodding. "Oh, yeah. We had a funeral for Harry the Sasquatch and everything. I think I remember where!" She leapt off the trail toward Fort Tidewell, kicking up dirt and loose stones that tumbled down the steep slope. John watched the mini-avalanches with a pinch of anxiety.

"Wait!" John said, but he only hesitated a moment before chasing after her.

They ran a little ways before Sarah suddenly skidded to a stop, holding her arms out to stop John behind her.

"What is it?" John asked, trying to see around her body.

"This wasn't here before," Sarah said.

John bobbed his head left and right but didn't see anything but scree and rocks and trees.

"What is it?" John asked. "Did you find a real Sasquatch?"

Sarah turned her body sideways so John could see, but she kept one arm out like a turnstile guarding him.

Up ahead, almost like an optical illusion in the rocks, a black oval dissolved into the mountain. It seemed to shimmer in the fading sunlight.

"What . . . is it?" John asked, taking a step back.

Sarah moved forward. "It—" She stepped closer, hunching to get a better look at the dark shape about the dimensions of the full-length mirror they had on the back of their bathroom door. "It looks like a cave. Cool!"

"Careful, Sarah. We shouldn't go in there."

"That's a great idea," Sarah said, standing upright and walking toward the mysterious black shape.

"No, wait, I said we *shouldn't* go in there." John turned to walk away. But he couldn't leave his sister. "We should get Mom and Dad."

"I'll just peek in," Sarah said, standing only an arm's length from the entrance. "It definitely looks like a cave, or maybe an old mining tunnel or something. I don't remember this from before."

"Come on, Sarah." John's tone sounded more urgent now.

Sarah stepped closer, slowly, her lips parted and her eyes fixed on the cave.

Without another word, Sarah stepped across the threshold, and her body disappeared into the black.

"Sarah!" John called out. "Sarah!" He pushed his foot into the ground for a running start toward where Sarah had been absorbed into the mountain. But he slipped on the loose gravel and his leg slid out from underneath him, pitching his body forward and onto the slope. He landed hard with a thump and a puff of dirt, the air knocked from his lungs.

John rolled down the rough hill, then splayed out and came to a rest on his back. He lay there, catching his breath, assessing the damage. Startled, but no pain. Trees above. Ground below. All good signs. He leaned forward and saw some scratches on his legs but no blood, no broken bones. Lots of dirt on his clothes, but that was normal when playing in the forest, so something he didn't think twice about. He shook his head and a cloud of dust billowed out, making him sneeze.

"John?" It was Sarah's voice. "You coming?"

John turned and looked uphill. Sarah's head and torso seemed suspended in midair, pushing out of the dark hole in the mountain like someone stick-ing out their tongue and saying *Ahhhhh*. She had a flashlight in one hand, waving him up. Sarah seemed to take no notice of his awkward sitting position down the hill.

"Just enjoying the view down here," John said.

"Well, stop lollygagging and get up here. Check this out! So cool!"

John stood and dusted himself off and was re-lieved he didn't have a twisted ankle or torn knee.

"Wow," he said to himself. "Got lucky that time." A jagged rock like a Native American hunt-ing knife stuck out from a boulder mere inches from where he'd tumbled down. If he'd slid across that, he might not have been so lucky.

John reached the tunnel. He couldn't see Sarah inside, but he cupped his hands over his mouth and shouted in. "I still don't think this is a good idea, Sarah. Come out. Let's get Dad and Mom to explore this with us. You know they say we shouldn't go spelunking without proper gear."

Sarah popped her head out of the void, startling John backward. His foot hit a rock at an awkward angle, and he was about to fall back down the slope again when Sarah's hand reached out and grabbed him by the shirt. For a moment he dangled backward, then pulled himself up to vertical.

"You mean proper gear like this?" Sarah said, flicking on and off her flashlight.

John really meant *parental supervision*, but he didn't want to tell that to his sixth-grade sister. No, wait—seventh-grade.

"I'm going whether you're coming or not," Sarah said. "Just a quick peek and then we'll catch up with Mom and Dad. Come on, it'll be fun!"

For the second time this evening, John's shoulders slumped and he put his head back, reluctant to accept that she was going no matter what he said. "Fine. But make it quick."

"Two minutes, promise. Yay!" Sarah disappeared into the tunnel.

John checked his watch: 6:52 p.m. He flipped on his flashlight and poked his head across the line of darkness. It wasn't particularly noisy outside, but once he stuck his head into the portal, sound seemed to get sucked away. It was a kind of quiet he'd never experienced.

The flashlight fought away the darkness, but

even its light seemed suppressed. John smacked it on the side, thinking maybe the battery was low.

When he aimed the beam back into the tunnel, Sarah's face appeared in an instant, sending a jolt of sheer panic up John's spine, and he jumped and dropped his light. What should have been the clatter of it falling into the ground sounded muted.

John saw Sarah's lips move and he could hear her faint whisper. It felt like he had cotton in his ears. He picked up his flashlight.

"What?" John asked, wiggling a pinky in his ear.

"Quiet in here," Sarah said, not really any louder than she had before, but closer to his ear.

"Yeah, it's weird," John shouted. "Isn't there usually an echo in a cave like this?"

"And that smell," she said, sniffing.

John took a snort of air. What was that smell? He closed his eyes and took another full inhale. A memory of the beach in California with his cousins came into his mind. Not the ocean, but when he'd been buried up to his neck in the sand. That smell of hot sand, not like dirt or silt or anything else—the smell of a zillion tiny rocks.

"Sand?" John asked, opening his eyes. But Sarah was gone. "Sarah?"

The dim beam from her flashlight danced up ahead, then turned a corner and disappeared.

"Sarah!" John yelled after her. "We shouldn't go any deeper! This isn't safe!"

John stood still, ears perked, waiting for a response. He couldn't even hear his own breathing. Sarah probably hadn't heard him. Or she'd decided not to respond.

A look back to the tunnel entrance reassured John. He was barely inside the cave, but it seemed so much darker than it should, as if light couldn't penetrate past the entrance. Leaning back out of the cave, he heard a flush of sound and he breathed in fresh mountain pine air. It calmed him. With a lungful of that, he straightened up and took a few more steps forward. After about ten steps, the passage veered to the right. Up ahead another five or six steps, he could see Sarah, her flashlight tracing over shapes on the wall.

John looked back to the cave entrance. It looked so far away, like the light just stopped immediately at the cave entrance. The rectangle of shimmering light sparkled so brilliantly bright compared to the darkness surrounding him. If he stepped further toward Sarah, he wouldn't have that touch point with the light; he wouldn't be able to see his exit.

A pressure weighed on his chest and pushed thick blood up into his neck that pounded through his temples. His breaths were harder to force. He'd just take the few steps to Sarah and drag her out. If she wouldn't come, then he'd go get their parents and tell them. Sure, she'd call him a tattletale, but this was too much. This—this was too much.

He didn't quite realize it until he got all the way to Sarah, but John had been holding his breath since losing sight of the exit. When he touched her arm, he exhaled heavy air and inhaled another lungful, though it felt like it only filled him up a quarter full at most.

"We have to go." He moaned the words like they could be his last.

"Look at this," Sarah said, amazement in her calm voice. She didn't seem to be suffering any of the same effects John endured. Her eyes were big round orbs staring at the wall in front of them.

John followed her gaze and looked at the wall. Into the stone, worn etchings depicted shapes and animals and what might be interpreted as letters, though not in English.

"It's so cool," Sarah said, transfixed. "Are these hieroglyphs?"

"You mean like from ancient Egypt?" John asked. Sarah's wonder had momentarily distracted him from his own panic, and his breathing had almost miraculously returned to normal.

"Ancient Egypt," Sarah repeated.

She stepped closer to the wall and traced one particular carving in the shape of an eye. It had two lines coming out from the bottom of it, one going straight down with a knifelike edge, another that stretched at an angle diagonal, with a curlicue finish.

As soon as her finger finished following the line of the eye, a bright flash illuminated the chamber for nothing more than the blip of a nanosecond, as if an electric bulb had exploded and gone out. John blinked back a sudden headache, wondering if he'd imagined the burst.

"Did you see that? So cool!" Sarah exclaimed.

John's heart was in his throat. "Can we get outta here now?"

"So cool," Sarah repeated, shaking her head. "I wish I had my phone to take a picture of this. Dad will love it!"

John tugged on Sarah's shirt. "Can we please go now, Sarah? Please?" He could feel sweat on his forehead.

"Yes, fine," Sarah said, pulling her arm away from his tugging. "This is a dead end, anyway. Let's go."

She marched off back to the corner and around it, John close behind. John could feel his chest loosening with every step, could almost taste the mountain air again. He plodded along behind her in the tunnel without looking up.

As soon as they were out of the cave, John smashed into the back of Sarah, who'd stopped suddenly.

"What the—" she muttered.

John didn't smell the fresh mountain air. When he looked around his sister, expecting to see the scree slope and forest and the way back to the trail, instead he dropped his flashlight and his jaw at the same time.

He'd never seen anything like it.

CHAPTER THREE

Sand, Sand, and More Sand in a Strange Land

JOHN

"Sarah, where are we?" John asked, frozen in place despite the heat. In front of them was a vast ocean of sand as far as the eye could see. It rolled in carved waves, dunes that sparkled in the low-slanting rays of the sun.

Dunes? John thought.

Sarah staggered forward, shielding her eyes from the glare. "I—I—"

It was rare for her to be speechless. And it was kind of spooky, her not saying anything and step-ping forward with the jerky movements of a zombie.

"Are you okay?" John followed his sister out into the sand, suddenly very afraid to be even a foot away from her.

"Woo-hoo!" she shouted, jumping into the air in her signature move, arms shooting up in a V shape.

"You're excited about this?" John snapped. "Sarah, how are we in a desert all of a sudden? Where's the mountain? The cave?" The incredible moment tickled at his brain, and he couldn't put two and two together. "Am I dreaming?"

"Yeah," Sarah said. "Dreaming. We must be dreaming. Together." She knelt into the sand, picked up a handful, and let it drain out of her fist. "This feels pretty real to me." She turned around to John as she said it, so he could see the roll of her eyes.

"How could we be in the mountains in one moment and then . . ." He trailed off, watching Sarah's eyes go up and her head tilt back, taking in something very large behind him. John wasn't sure he wanted to turn around.

Sarah laughed, her face turned toward the sky,

her hand covering her mouth. "So." She took a full breath. "Cool!"

The curiosity got the better of him. John held his breath and rotated on his heels in the sand. He'd been stunned by the vast golden dunes, but what he saw now made him squeak out a chortle of disbelief.

"What—? How—? Is that—?" John stammered. His finger reached out, pointing to the scene as if maybe he could poke it, like it was a postcard of a giant pyramid and not a real one.

"A pyramid," Sarah said, awestruck.

"A pyramid," John repeated, more a question than a statement, asking himself if it was real. He'd heard his dad use the word "flabbergasted" a few times before, and it seemed to accurately sum up the state of utter astonishment he felt now. John blinked his eyes, hoping the illusion would disappear. *Flabbergasted.*

John moved his head to look at Sarah. Only at the last degree of his head's slow rotation did he take his eyes off the huge stepped-stone structure. Then he swallowed hard. This couldn't be real. No, this couldn't be real. "I'm kinda freakin' out here, sis. What's happening? Where *are* we?"

Sarah shrugged her shoulders up and held them there, her head ticking back and forth like a slow metronome, obviously in shock. "Egypt?"

"Egypt?" John asked, incredulous. "There's no way we could be in Egypt. Something happened . . . When I fell down the hill, yes! I must've hit my head. I'm unconscious and dreaming. Obviously dreaming. That's all this is." He chuckled a nervous laugh. "I have to be—"

"Look." Sarah pointed to a small rectangle in the base of the pyramid. About the size of the mirror that hung on the back of their bathroom door, the doorway was edged with freshly etched hieroglyphs. Set back into the stone on either side, a statue of a woman with a scorpion on her head stood guard. The quality of the material made it appear practically brand-new.

"Is that where we came out?" Sarah asked. "From the cave?"

"What? That can't be," John replied in a knee-jerk reaction. "This is just a dream."

Sarah cocked her head and looked at him in response. "A dream?"

"Yeah, this is a dream," John reiterated. "I'll wake up any minute now and have a good lump on my head, and it'll be fine because we're not in Egypt. We can't be, that's impossible."

Sarah seemed to ignore the rant and instead scanned their surroundings. John watched her eyes stop to stare at something on their left. He couldn't help but look too.

Beyond the edge of the pyramid, shimmering on the near horizon, it looked like palm trees and a village of squat houses, wavering as if a mirage. Turning a bit farther, John could see a huge river winding away over the horizon.

"This is quite a dream," John muttered under his breath.

"Over there." Sarah pointed. A brown-skinned boy, barefoot and bare chested, wearing a white kilt-like wrapping around his hips and thighs, walked away from the river holding a large clay jug. He moved toward the village.

"Hey!" Sarah yelled.

"Shush!" John hissed. "We don't know him." He immediately felt silly for reacting that way. What did it matter, if this was only a dream? But John's chest grew heavy, anxiety weighing him down regardless. He'd never had a dream so elaborate as this. He was starting to consider that maybe it was, in fact, not a dream. His brain ached admitting the possibility.

Sarah laughed. "Aw, come on. He's just some kid. Maybe he can help us figure out what happened." She ran off toward him, but it was slow going through the sand. John hesitated, feeling immobilized by the what-ifs. His fear of being left alone won out, and after a heavy sigh, he trudged after his sister.

As soon as the boy caught sight of them, he stopped in his tracks and gave them a strange look.

"Stop!" the boy said, taking a few steps back and putting the clay jug in front of himself almost as a shield. "Who are you?"

If this really was Egypt, John was surprised that he could understand the boy. What language did they speak in Egypt, anyway? The fact that it didn't seem to matter? Add it to the growing list of oddities. And another: Why wasn't this boy wearing a modern pair of shorts? Is this how they still dress in Egypt?

"I can understand you," Sarah said, obviously having similar thoughts as John about their ability to communicate.

"And I can understand you," the boy said, his narrowed eyes conveying distrust while also be-dazzled by the flashes off Sarah's glittery sequined shirt. "But who are you?"

"I'm Sarah. And he's—" She gestured to John.

"I'm very confused," John said.

"He's John," Sarah said, rolling her eyes.

"Sarah," the boy repeated. "And John. Uh-huh." His dark brown eyes tried to catch John's. The boy still didn't move the jug or change his feet from their defensive position, as if he was getting ready to wrestle. "I'm Zachariah, son of Imhotep."

"Howdy, Zack," Sarah said, thrusting her hand out to shake.

Zack winced in his defensive posture. After apparently assessing that it wasn't an attack, he gave her outstretched hand a questioning look. "Where are you from? And what're you doing here?"

"Well." Sarah retracted her hand. "That's a very

good question. Can you tell us where 'here' is, exactly?"

Zack moved his gaze up to her face, his brow furrowed and his face scrunched up as if she'd just asked the funniest thing in the world. "This is Saqqara, land of King Djoser." He gestured around with his head.

"King Joe-sir," Sarah repeated, nodding.

"Yes, King Djoser," Zack said, nodding with her.

They both nodded a few more times together, eyeing each other. Watching them in unison, John felt himself suddenly nodding along too. It went on for a few odd moments, everyone nodding together.

Then Zack stopped his head from bobbing and asked again, "Where'd you say you're from?"

"We're not in Kansas anymore," John said to Sarah, making a reference to *The Wizard of Oz* movie, when Dorothy woke up in a fantastical land after getting sucked up into a tornado. She eventually escaped the magical land of Oz in a hot air balloon. If he wasn't going to wake up soon in a hospital in Colorado from hitting his head, John hoped they'd find an easier way home than by hot air balloon.

"Does that make him a Munchkin?" Sarah kicked her thumb over at Zack, alluding to the inhabitants of Oz. John let out one dazed chuckle. This all still seemed too unreal to fathom, but, just as it had sunken in with Dorothy, John could feel his mind coming to terms with it, whether he liked it or not. Exactly what "it" was that he was coming to realize still seemed foggy.

Zack watched their exchange with a wrinkled forehead. "You two are strange."

"Well," Sarah said, one hand on her hip. "That's kind of rude." But she smiled after the mock offense.

"Why are you here?"

"Just traveling through," Sarah said with a smirk. "Kind of by accident, really. I take it you don't see many people like us?"

"I've never seen anyone like you," Zack said, his eyebrows shooting up. "Your clothes are—I've never seen that type of *shendyt*." Zack pointed at John's loose gray shorts that weren't all that different from the fabric wrapped around his own waist. "Or a woman not wearing a *kalasiris*. Why do you wear that odd shendyt when you should be wearing a dress?" He gestured to Sarah's jean-colored stretch pants.

"Excuse me?" Sarah put both hands on her hips and cocked one side out at an angle. "Girls don't have to wear dresses all the time, you know."

Zack raised one eyebrow, seemingly befuddled by Sarah's attitude. "Where'd you say you're from?"

"Colorado," John said.

"Never heard of it," Zack said.

"United States?" Sarah added.

Zack shook his head.

John wiped the back of his hand across the sweat that had suddenly sprouted on his forehead. This wasn't feeling right. How could someone not have heard of the good ol' U.S. of A.?

"What is that bracelet?" Zack pointed to John's arm with a finger, his hand still clasping the jug. With the movement, John heard water sloshing inside.

"This?" John asked, pointing at his watch.

"Yeah, is that cowhide?" Zack stepped closer.

This was getting weirder by the second. First

this boy is dressed in a cloth kilt, then he doesn't know about America, now he doesn't recognize a watch? Was Egypt really so far behind the times?

John held out his arm, going along with Zack's request to see it, but thoroughly confused. He could smell tangy sweat and sweet incense on the boy. "Cowhide? It's plastic. It's a Timex. It's—"

John tapped on the face, looking for the time. It was frozen at 6:55 p.m. and 48 seconds.

"Timex?" Zack asked. "Is that a form of onyx? What are those markings?"

John tapped on his watch face again. The seconds didn't change. Still stuck at 48. "Sarah, look," he said, tapping harder on the watch.

"What am I looking at?" Sarah said, holding his forearm.

"The time. It's frozen!" John said, shaking his wrist.

"So? Your watch is broken. Ask for a new one for Christmas."

"It shows 6:55 and 48 seconds, but it should be 6:56 by now. At least." Sure, it could only be broken, but John sensed that it meant something more. All the pieces that would reveal their true situation were swirling in his head; he just had to put them together.

Zack scrunched up his face again. "It's like a shadow clock?"

"What's a shadow clock?" Sarah asked.

John didn't see how that had anything to do with anything.

"You know, a shadow clock," Zack said. "To tell time."

"How's it work?" Sarah asked. John could feel his impatience burning through his forehead. Why did this matter right now?! Didn't they have more important problems? He wiped his sweaty brow again.

Zack looked at Sarah as if she were from a different planet.

Not quite another planet, but maybe something like that, John thought.

"You know," Zack said. "An obelisk. Sun shines on it. Casts a shadow." He explained it as if they were in kindergarten.

"Like a sundial," Sarah said. Zack shook his head as if he'd never heard the term.

Sarah continued, "An obelisk must be a piece of

metal or something?"

"Metal?" Zack shook his head and sniggered. Not knowing an obelisk was comical? "You know. An obelisk. A tower, a pillar, where we write all our legends. You must've seen an obelisk before. Maybe you just don't call it that? In your land—Call-oh-raw-doe—how do you represent the mound that Atum stood on at the creation of the world?"

"Uhhhh" was all that John could say, so many questions dog piled on top of one another in his mind. They definitely weren't in Kansas anymore. John was realizing that Kansas—or Colorado—may not even exist where they were now. Or *when* they were now. It left him speechless.

A wave of paranoia flashed through John like a firecracker. The idea that they'd traveled not only to Egypt, but to *ancient* Egypt?! Ludicrous. Ridiculous.

Ridiculous!

Why hadn't they immediately gone right back into the portal they'd come out? What if it only stayed "open" to the other side for a finite amount of time? He must have been in shock and not thinking clearly and blindly following Sarah. Of course, she loved this sort of adventure regardless of the consequences.

How could he have been so—so—*stupid*! Yes, he used *that* word.

John wiped the back of his hand again across the sweat that now drenched his forehead. He could feel a clarity in his thoughts, and it was plain what they had to—

"We have to go," John said, tugging on Sarah's shirt. "We have to go, Sarah. Now. Back through the door." He pointed to the pyramid.

"I don't want to," Sarah said.

"We have to get out of here," John pleaded. "Before it's too late!"

"I want to check this place out," she replied, cool as a cucumber. "Don't you realize where we are?"

"The door," John pointed. "What if it closes?"

"That door?" Zack asked, pointing to the same door John was pointing at.

John's finger trembled. "Yes."

"That's a false door," Zack said.

"What?" John could feel the color drain from his face.

"For the *ka* of the king."

"Ka?" John repeated, feeling his brain go numb again. Had the portal closed already? Was he hallucinating, imagining that there was a portal to ancient Egypt in the cave behind his house? He shook his head. He must be unconscious back in Colorado right now. Must be. This was all some bizarre dream. Had to be. Yep. A dream. Ancient Egypt, ha!

"That's, like, the soul, I think," Sarah said. "My friend Cynthia went to a Cirque du Soleil show called *Kà*. I didn't know what it meant, so I looked it up."

Sarah was a proud Word Nerd, but did she not understand the severity of their situation? Was now a time to learn a new word? They had to go!

"Then," Sarah went on, "she told me the play was something totally different. But I still learned some really interesting stuff."

Zack nodded, one eye permanently cocked. John felt frozen, watching the scene as if he were apart from it, as if it were a television show.

Sarah continued, "I went down an etymology rabbit hole."

"Edda-what?" Zack asked.

"Etymology. The origin of words," Sarah said, smiling. John knew she enjoyed sharing that definition. Ever since she learned it last year, she never hesitated to bust it out when the opportunity presented itself. "Anyway, ka is as real as a living being. I mean, that's what you believe, right, Zack?"

Zack nodded as if he'd been asked if rain comes from the sky.

"Just like we do, the ka needs air," Sarah continued, "and to get out from time to time, stretch its legs, catch some rays. That's why the door."

"So it's *not* fake?" John asked.

"It's real. For the ka." Sarah chuckled. John had no idea how she could find any of this amusing. "And when inside the pyramid, the ka needs food and such to survive." Looking at Zack, she went on, "So you pack bread and honey in the burial chamber with the king like he's going on a long journey. Servants too, right? Kinda freaky—"

Sarah stopped talking. Zack stared at her aghast.

"You don't believe in ka?" Zack asked, as if he'd never met such a person.

John took Sarah by the elbow. "I need to talk to you. Alone." He tugged her away.

"I should probably get going," Zack said, still eyeing them oddly. "So long!"

"Wait!" Sarah called back. "Just wait one minute. Please."

"Uh," Zack groaned, but he didn't leave.

Far enough away to be out of Zack's earshot, John whispered, "Sarah, do you realize what's happened? I mean, I'm still really hoping that I hit my head and am dreaming all this. But on the off chance that's not true, do you understand where we are?"

"Of course," she replied.

"And when?"

"I get it, John. Ancient Egypt. Isn't it amazing?"

John's jaw dropped. "How—how can you be so accepting about this?"

"We're like Neil Armstrong and Buzz Aldrin landing on the moon. Can you imagine how famous we'll be? This is the adventure of a lifetime, John! Soak it up while you can!"

John's cheeks heated up. "But—"

"But nothing, John. Live a little."

His cheeks flared to red-hot. "How do we get home, Sarah?"

"Don't know." She leaned her head back. "But we'll figure it out. We always do. Don't worry so much."

"You need to worry more!" John blurted. "What if we're stuck here forever?"

"I highly doubt that's the case—"

"Based on what?" John yelled.

"Gut feeling," she replied. "But look, even if we are stuck here, no sense worrying about it, right? Does worrying about it get us home? Or—think about it—maybe the way we get home is to try and understand what happened, understand things like ka, learn more about that pyramid and how to get inside. Maybe that's our ticket back."

John didn't have a response. She'd hit on a grain of truth there. They had no idea how they'd traveled here, except that they'd somehow walked through a door through time from a cave in the mountains. Maybe Sarah was right. Maybe if they learned more about this place, and this pyramid, they could figure out the secret of the portal—and a way back home.

Sarah broke the silence. "You know I'm right." Then she put her arm on her brother's shoulder. "It'll be all right, Johnny. Trust me."

John huffed. "Do I have a choice?"

Sarah gave him a tight hug. "That's the spirit!"

They both turned and walked back toward Zack, Sarah with her arm around her brother's shoulders. John had to admit to himself that her confidence and hug were somewhat comforting. The anxiety still gnawed at him, but she was right.

There was nothing that worrying could do about it.

"Well," Zack said, "I really need to get going. My mother and father are expecting me. It's been, um, interesting to meet you."

"Look, Zack," Sarah said, speaking as she might when revealing a secret. "I'll be honest. We need help. We're sort of—"

"Lost," John finished her sentence, and the word never felt more true.

"Yeah," Sarah said. "And we could really use some help. Would it be too much trouble if we tagged along with you? You said your dad is Imhotep, right?"

"That's right," Zack said, not immediately accepting Sarah's self-invite.

"And he's the architect of this pyramid, right?" Sarah asked. Had she learned that from the Egyptology unit she took last year in sixth grade?

"That's right." Zack nodded, acting both proud of this fact and wary of this line of questioning.

"We're big fans," John said.

"Big fans," Sarah repeated. "And we'd love to learn more about the pyramid."

"We'd be thrilled," John said.

Zack's shoulders lowered and a half smile cracked his lips. "Oh, you admire my father's work?"

"We do," Sarah said. "And we want to learn more."

"Absolutely," John agreed.

"Well, why didn't you say that to begin with?" Zack asked, a full smile on his lips now. "I love to talk about the pyramid. As does my father. Did you know I work on it too?"

"Really?" Sarah replied.

"Listen," Zack said. He paused, thinking about something for a few seconds. Then, blushing slightly, he asked, "How about—would you like to come to my house for dinner?"

Sarah's face lit up and she looked at John with a beaming smile.

"Are you sure?" she asked Zack.

Zack's cheeks flared. "Yeah. We're having tilapia stew with barley. My mom makes the best in Saqqara. At least that's what my dad says."

"Great! Thank you so much," Sarah said, moving closer to Zack and patting him on the shoulder. "Need some help with that jug?"

Zack chuckled and turned toward the village. "Welcome to Saqqara."

Walking through the deep sand, John felt a little like he was walking on the moon. Just like Neil Armstrong and Buzz Aldrin.

They entered the village of Saqqara by walking underneath a whitewashed arch etched with hieroglyphs John didn't understand. So they could understand each other's language when speaking but couldn't read the writing? Time-travel rules were so confusing.

A gray short-haired dog loped up alongside them. John patted its head and the dog licked his rough tongue across John's fingers. To the left of the road, a fenced-in pen held about a dozen head of cattle. Next to that, sheep, then a muddier area for pigs. The smell of dung assaulted John's nostrils.

They walked past whitewashed mud-brick houses with brown wooden doors. John could see inside a few of them. In one, a gray-haired woman hunched over a large stone bowl, holding a stone rod and grinding something with steady movements of her wrinkled arms. A jeweled ring on her finger caught the sun and winked at John. In another, a naked toddler played on a reed mat on the dirt. The mother came to the open door and half shut it, but stopped when she saw John and Sarah walking in the street, especially entranced by the glitter of Sarah's sequined shirt.

A middle-aged man holding a string of fish and a harpoon walked by in bare feet and a white shendyt—John noticed the linen kilt was common on all the men—his eyes locked on Sarah's bedazzling shirt.

"I think we're going to need some new clothes," John whispered to his sister.

"How long are you staying?" Zack asked. "My mom might have something you can borrow, Sarah. And I have extra for you, John."

"That is so nice of you," Sarah said, touching Zack's shoulder and putting one hand over her heart.

Zack's cheeks flared again. John wondered if Zack might be interested in his sister. They might be similar ages. *Oh, great.*

"You work on the pyramid?" John asked, pushing in between Zack and Sarah as they strolled together.

"That's right," Zack said, pushing out his chest with pride.

"How long?" Sarah asked.

"Well, I've been working as a scribe for the past year—" They turned a corner and saw a one-legged man sitting on the side of the road with a wicker dish in front of him. Zack bowed.

As they moved on, Zack whispered, "The pyramid can be dangerous work."

"He lost his leg working on the pyramid?" John asked.

"He was lucky it was only his leg," Zack said. "Some have died."

They walked together a few more paces in silence.

"But," Zack continued, "my father has been working safely on the pyramid for thirty years. He's the architect, as you mentioned, Sarah. He's also the vizier to King Djoser."

"Vizier?" Sarah asked, her Word Nerd hunger wanting to be fed.

Surprising to John, Zack didn't respond with yet another slanted eyebrow and confused look. It seemed he was settling into the fact that John and Sarah weren't from around here.

"Um, like a counselor, an advisor," Zack said. "Like Thoth is to Ra."

"Okay." Sarah nodded. "Thoth?"

"God of writing." Zack grinned. "Among other things."

"And Ra?" Sarah asked.

With his chin, Zack gestured to the sun, which hung close to the horizon, and blinked into it. "Ra.

Creator of all things. Ruler of the sky, the earth, and the underworld."

"Ra," John repeated, pointing at the sun. "The sun."

"Son? Like I am to my father?" Zack asked.

"No, the sun, s-u-n, like the sun in the sky. Ra."

Zack smiled. "Ah, so you do know this god. You call him Sun. We call him Ra." He nodded slightly, gazing at John. "Amazing. I want to ask you so many questions about Call-oh-raw-doe."

They wound through worn streets, the homes getting bigger. John saw a man and a woman watching them from the roof of one three-story building. The woman looking down wore a green head scarf, which contrasted richly with her straight black hair.

"That's our house up there," Zack said, pointing to the biggest house in the village, atop a slight hill. "My mom and dad probably wonder where I am."

Zack mentioning his parents gave John a pang in his heart. He leaned to Sarah and whispered, "Think Mom and Dad are worried about us too?"

"Maybe," Sarah said. "But not much we can do

about other people's worry, is there?" She gave a consoling grin. "We'll see them soon. Promise."

"If you don't have a place to sleep tonight," Zack said, "you can probably stay with us. I'd have to ask my parents, of course, but we have guest rooms."

Sarah held out her hands palms up to John, like *How can we refuse?*

John swallowed the lump in his throat. This was all so unreal. Maybe a good sleep and he'd wake up in the hospital back in Colorado. Or, even better, maybe he'd wake up back in his own bed.

Besides being much bigger, the front of Zack's house was relatively plain like the others: a brown door set in a whitewashed wall. But what was different was the number of windows. Apparently having windows was a sign of wealth. Imhotep was an architect, after all.

John stepped in through the front door after Zack and Sarah, and his eyes grew wide. "Whoa," he muttered.

Zack stood aside and gestured to an expansive open courtyard filled with fruit trees and lush green plants and a lovely pool of aquamarine water, surrounded by colorful flowers in full bloom. Columns lined the edges of the yard, which skirted a hallway leading off into other rooms. Unlike the other homes John had seen, this house made frequent use of a beautiful white stone.

"That looks like the rock I saw on the pyramid," John said.

"That's right," Zack said. "Limestone. Mined from a quarry not far from here."

A woman appeared, walking toward them. She wore a tube-shaped dress patterned like bright fish scales of green and gold, two broad straps extending behind her neck. Woven sandals on her feet. A shawl of sheer linen draped over her shoulders, her black hair pulled back, her dark eyes accentuated by darker makeup.

"There you are!" she exclaimed, holding her hands out toward Zack. "I need that water for our dinner." She paused, eyeing John with a quick once-over, then lingering on Sarah and her glittery shirt. "And who are your new friends?"

"This—" Zack started.

"I'm Sarah," she said, sticking out her hand.

The woman's smooth skin wrinkled slightly between her eyebrows. "Your clothes are—I don't know about those leggings, but that top half is—incredible."

"They're from a land called Call-oh-raw-doe," Zack said. "And you should have seen the looks we got walking through the village. I told her maybe she could borrow something from you?"

"Of course, of course," the woman said. "Travelers, eh? Wonderful. We love visitors. My name is Hatmehit. Welcome to my home."

"Thank you," John said. Really all he wanted to do was go lay down and hope to wake up from this dream. He yawned.

"Tired from a hard day's travel?" Hatmehit asked. "What's your name?"

"John," he said. "Tidewell."

"Well, John-Tidewell, I'll make a bed up for you," Hatmehit said. "But how about some dinner first? Do you like tilapia barley stew?"

John realized he was hungry. It didn't seem that long ago he'd wolfed down herb-roasted chicken and green beans and potatoes with his own family, but it also seemed like a lifetime ago. Thinking about it, his stomach growled. Guess time travel makes you hungry too.

"That'd be great," he replied.

Sarah nearly cracked her cheeks from grinning so broadly. "Can't wait. I love trying new things. Love it."

"We'll get you some new clothes, then you can help me in the kitchen," Hatmehit said, putting a hand on Sarah's back and ushering her toward a side hall.

Sarah looked back at John. She knew she wasn't the cook between them.

"Come on," Zack said. "I'll show you my room and get you some new clothes too."

John didn't move, watching his sister disappear. He suddenly felt a twist in his gut, like he was more alone than ever. But he looked over at Zack and gave a tepid tip of his head. "Thanks."

Zack seemed to pick up on John's feelings. "I think you're gonna like it here." He smiled warmly.

Hopefully, not for long, John thought.

CHAPTER FOUR

A Dinner Proposal

JOHN

John sat at a wooden table that could host twelve, along with Sarah, Zack, and Zack's parents. He wafted the steamy aroma of the tilapia barley stew toward his nose, something his mom had taught him how to do when they cooked together. He grinned thinking of her nickname for him: *Little Chef*.

Thinking of her, his mother's voice popped into his head telling him to get dressed for dinner. John now wore the white linen kilt called the shendyt, borrowed from Zack, and—as was the ancient

Egyptians' custom—he was bare chested.

"Wow," John said for the second time. "This is delicious. Earthy, but spicy." He'd heard his mom describe a chili that way once. "I have to get this recipe from you, Mrs.—" John wasn't sure what to call her. She'd only introduced herself as Hatmehit, not Mrs. Hatmehit. John gave a shy smile to Zack's mother.

The woman grinned at John. "It's the finest tilapia from the Nile River. Plus green onion and barley. But there are two additional, important ingredients . . ." She let it dangle, building up the anticipation.

Sarah slurped up another spoonful.

John leaned forward. "Yes?"

"Water from the Nile, of course. But!" Hatmehit held up a finger. "It must be drawn near sunset. That is where you met our Zachariah." She stroked the short dark hair of her son. "And the secret ingredient—do you promise not to tell?" She gave a mischievous grin and bent over the table to whisper.

"Promise," John said, barely whispering himself, entranced by the woman's delivery. He absentmindedly pulled another spoonful up to his lips as she revealed the secret.

"Garlic." She clapped her hands and leaned back, as if it were both a simple and amazing revelation. "Coarsely ground and sprinkled into the stew about three-quarters of the way through the process. Don't add it too early!" She shook her finger. "And certainly not too late."

"Timing is everything. Isn't it, my dear?" Zack's father, Imhotep, spoke with a commanding voice.

"Timing is everything," Hatmehit repeated with a smile, extending her hand to her husband. Imhotep took her hand and kissed the back of it.

"Just like our pyramid," Imhotep said. "It will be completed right on time. On the day of the summer solstice."

"That's the longest day of the year," Zack added, looking to Sarah and John. "When we celebrate the longest day of Ra."

"We're glad to have you for a visit, Sarah and John of Call-oh-raw-doe," Imhotep said. "Is your land on the other side of the Nile?"

"Um, I guess you could say that," Sarah responded, hardly suppressing a giggle.

"Is it beyond the Great Green Sea?" the man asked, putting down his spoon.

"We've traveled very far to get here, yes," John said.

"I've only heard stories about the other side," Imhotep said, his mind seeming to wander. "What good fortune! The gods must have sent you to us. Because once this pyramid is complete, after thirty long years, we'll be moving to live across the Great Green Sea. I've accepted a commission on the other side." He smiled and shook a fist as if he'd won a victory. "I should like to learn from you about your customs to ready us for the move."

John noticed that Zack let out a groan when Imhotep mentioned the move.

His mother noticed too. "Come now, Zachariah. We've talked about this. You'll be fine. And you'll get to work on an even bigger and better pyramid than the one in Saqqara."

"That's what you tell me," Zack said, head down sulking. "But my friends are here."

"You'll make new ones," Hatmehit said. "I know it."

"Shared experience and time, son," Imhotep said. "That's what bonds people together in friendship. In time, I trust you'll make good friends across the Great Green Sea just as you have here in Saqqara."

"Whatever," Zack said. John couldn't help but think of his own friend, Roman. They'd shared a thousand experiences together. Was that all it was, shared experience and time? He pictured Roman laughing in his goofy, endearing way and it made John grin. Every time.

Ignoring Zack's glib remark, Imhotep brought the subject back to the move and his new project. "I've learned a great deal from this pyramid, but since it was the first one of its kind, there are things I intend to do differently for the next. For example, I've designed a new way to create smooth diagonal lines up the sides of the pyramid, not like the steps you can see in this particular construction." He gestured out the open window of their second-floor dining room, out over the adjacent rooftops to the pyramid beyond, only the outline visible since the sun had set. "And I imag-ine glorious white marble reflecting Ra's light for miles around." He stared out the window, but John saw him looking into the future at his own design.

John could almost see it through Imhotep's eyes, a pearl-white pyramid shining like a brilliant jewel amid the golden sand. "People would come from all around the world to see it."

"A beacon of light," Sarah said, then whispering sideways to John: "Sound familiar?" With her nudging, John saw clearly in his mind's eye the bright flash of light that had strobed in the cave before they realized they'd traveled through time.

Zack groaned, loud enough to draw attention. His face was down, hidden, while he sipped on his soup with a carved wooden spoon, the handle shaped like a rabbit stretched and running.

Hatmehit scowled in Zack's direction and changed the subject. "Doesn't Sarah look lovely in that dress, Zack?"

Zack choked, then spurt a bit of the soup from his mouth back into the bowl. John rolled his eyes. His sister did look beautiful in the snug green dress Hatmehit had loaned to her. The subtle mossy color of the fabric made Sarah's red hair look all the more vibrant and fiery.

Sarah must have seen John roll his eyes. "Just cuz girls don't *have* to wear a dress doesn't mean we can't when we want to."

"You look great," John said, in all sincerity. "Maybe a little too old, though."

"Are you married, Sarah?" Imhotep asked, casually taking another spoonful of stew.

It was Sarah's turn to choke on her dinner. After she wiped her mouth and saw that Imhotep was serious, she answered with a polite "no."

"Zack is nearing that age," Imhotep said. "Perhaps I might speak with your parents about a prenuptial gift exchange."

"Dad!" Zack barked.

"Dear," Hatmehit said, placing a hand on her husband's forearm resting on the table. "Let's not embarrass Zachariah. We could discuss this directly with their parents, but—" Turning to Sarah and John, she frowned. "But I fear your parents are no longer with us, are they?"

"They're not here, if that's what you mean," Sarah said.

"I suspected you were orphans. Why else would

you be traveling alone so far from home?" Hatmehit shook her head and made a *tsk, tsk* sound. "I'm sorry."

"Oh, they're alive," John piped in. "Back home."

"Colorado," Sarah said.

"And they let you travel all alone across the Great Green Sea?" Imhotep asked, raising an eyebrow.

"I think there's more to this story," Hatmehit said, her tone seeming to agree with her husband's skepticism. "Did you run away?"

"Not exactly—" John said, looking to Sarah for help.

"We got separated," Sarah said. "An accident."

"A shipwreck," Imhotep concluded. "Such voyages can be dangerous."

"Yeah," John agreed quickly. "They survived, though, I know it."

Imhotep and Hatmehit exchanged a glance.

"That's why you didn't have any other clothes or luggage," Hatmehit added. "Oh, you poor dears."

"It's been very scary," John said, in all honesty. "I miss my mom and dad, my best friend, my house . . ." John hung his head to hide the tears he felt welling up in his eyes. "I'd really like to go home."

Next thing he knew, with his eyes closed, John felt a warm body hugging him. Not from his sister, but from Hatmehit. She held him and slowly stroked his hair. John remembered back to shooing his dad away from rubbing his hair, and he wished that someday he'd get a chance to let his dad have at it. The thought made him smile while a tear rolled down his cheek.

With the emotional end to dinner, John felt exhausted. He and Sarah stood from the table and thanked Hatmehit for the wonderful meal. They also expressed their gratitude to the parents for giving them a bed in which to sleep, and to Zack for offering in the first place.

"Rest well, children. Tomorrow is a big day!" Imhotep said.

Walking down the hallway, John asked Zack what his father meant by that.

"About tomorrow being a big day? He says that every night," Zack said. "Only a few more weeks of construction on the pyramid, so he's very excited to meet the deadline, as you heard." Zack paused, then added with a flinch of his shoulder: "But once it's done, we have to move, so I hope it takes forever."

John thought of his own family's impending move to Maryland. If they ever got back to Colorado, that is.

"Anyway," Zack said, changing his frown into a sneaky grin like he had a surprise for them, "you get to work with us tomorrow!"

"Work on the pyramid?" John asked, stopping in his tracks, remembering the one-legged man.

"That's right. Isn't it great?" Zack said. "Not everyone gets that honor."

"I'm up for it," Sarah replied.

It sounded like hard work to John.

"So yeah, get your rest. Here's your room," Zack said.

"Good night," Sarah said. "Thanks for everything, Zack." She gave him a quick hug.

Zack stammered, "Welcome—you're welcome. I

mean, yeah, no problem." He shrugged one shoulder. It looked like he was trying hard not to look like he was trying hard to play it cool.

John pushed his sister into the room.

"See you in the morning!" Zack waved to Sarah.

"G'night, Zachariah," John mumbled, closing the door in Zack's face.

The bed frames were of sturdy construction, with reeds woven across the slats to create a surface like a box spring. Cushions of soft material—was it wool?—felt as soft as a cloud to John's weary body. The day's mental flip-flops had tuckered him out. He pulled the delicate linen sheets up to his chin and looked out the open window, trying not to imagine the backbreaking labor of building a pyramid the next day.

The stars sprinkled throughout the sky popped as clear as if John and Sarah were camping on a cloudless night. John had seen stars smeared across the universe like this before, but never from the midst of civilization. They were in a village now, so why—

The answer occurred to him.

"No light pollution," John said out loud. He

leaned forward to see his sister across the room, but Sarah was already asleep.

CHAPTER FIVE

Into the Dark, and the Light

JOHN

The next day, John awoke to a slight chill in the air. Looking out the window, he saw an early-morning mist hanging low over the village like a cozy blanket. Still in ancient Egypt, he hadn't woken up from this strange dream. John pulled the warm sheets up to his chin and realized that something had been placed at the foot of his bed. At that moment, Zack came in wearing a long shirt that went down to his knees, a leather belt cinching it snug around his waist. A strip of leather around his neck disappeared under the collar—a necklace.

"You up?" Zack asked.

"I am—" John said, yawning.

"Might be a little cold for the shendyt this morning," Zack said, referring to the linen kilt they'd been wearing bare chested. "So I thought you might want a tunic. Like mine." He pointed to the clothes on John's bed. On top of the tunic coiled a leather belt wound like a snake. The tunic matched the one Zack wore.

"Thanks," John muttered, rubbing his eyes.

Zack walked to the window. "This fog will burn off soon."

John looked out at the light gray, the sun trying to push through, like they were living in a cloud city.

"Well," Zack said, tapping the windowsill. "Breakfast is ready, so I'll meet you in there."

John grunted as Zack left the room.

John stretched and yawned and enjoyed the soft bed a few more minutes, then he hoisted his body out of its comfort and pulled on the tunic. Made from a heavier material than the light shendyt, it felt warm, but at the same time airy and loose and comfortable. Looking down at himself, he couldn't help but feel a little embarrassment, the comparison to a dress being obvious. John had never worn a dress, but—hey, he could see why they were comfortable. And it wasn't all that different than the skirt-like kilt—the shendyt—he'd worn yesterday. If Roman could see him now . . .

John's stomach growled.

In the kitchen, Sarah and Zack were chatting and eating breakfast: a dark slab of bread drizzled with honey, and dates. John dug in. The bread tasted denser and more satisfying than any store-bought loaf John had ever eaten at home.

"What is this bread made from?" John asked.

"Farro," Hatmehit said. "Do you not have farro where you come from?"

"I don't know," John said, looking at Sarah. "Maybe at Whole Foods?"

Sarah giggled.

Hatmehit wrapped their lunch in a cloth—cured fish, dried apricots, celery, and another slice of farro bread.

"Don't you have school?" Sarah asked Zack.

Zack made a funny face and looked at his mother.

"You know," John said, "the place where you learn things. But mostly play with your friends."

"I've been to school, yes, when I was younger. My friends and I all work on the pyramid now. And we learn new things every day. Useful things. Like geometry, for example."

"You learned how to read in school," his mother piped in. "Don't forget that important skill."

"And write," Zack said proudly. "And now my father allows me on the team of carvers who write the inscriptions in the pyramid. I want to be a scribe as my profession."

"You mean the hieroglyphs?" John asked.

"I love writing," Zack said, his tone taking on a sense of wonder. "It's like—I mean, I can imagine something in my head, write it down, then you can read it sometime later and imagine the same thing without hearing me say it. Isn't that—"

"Magic?" Sarah interrupted.

"Yes, magic," Zack said. "Exactly."

"Time travel?" John added under his breath, thinking back to the hieroglyphs they saw in the cave before they were transported to ancient Egypt. What was the connection between those hieroglyphs, that flash of light, and their trip here? Wasn't there a specific design Sarah had touched? It felt like another clue forming on the tip of his tongue—

"It's wonderful," Hatmehit said. "Zack is quite the storyteller. Why don't you show them some of your fine handiwork at the pyramid today?"

"I think my mom is trying to tell us it's time to go," Zack said, smiling back at his mother.

"Have fun!" Hatmehit said as they left.

"Off to work on a pyramid. Awesome!" Sarah tried to skip through the sand. It was slow going, but that didn't dull her enthusiasm.

John didn't share her glee about the work, but he *was* eager to pull on the thread he'd been thinking about that might get them back home. Something with those hieroglyphs and that flash of light . . .

John inhaled deeply. The cool morning air smelled surprisingly moist, more like the lake they camped at as a family than the desert. He loved thinking about that gorgeous alpine lake, but it made him miss the fragrant smell of the forest back home. The desert lacked that piney scent.

Since his eyes were closed while he took another big whiff of the invigorating breeze, John didn't see the rock protruding from the sand, and he smashed his toe, then went tumbling down onto all fours. As he fell, his knuckle scraped a rock that felt oddly cold.

"John!" Sarah screamed. He hadn't hurt himself that bad; John didn't know why Sarah needed to scream about it.

"Don't move," Zack said, a sense of urgency in his voice John had never heard before.

John raised his head to see a brown-scaled snake, with a flared neck like it had swallowed a skinny Ping-Pong paddle, staring its black beady eyes at John's face.

"Don't move," Zack repeated. "Hold on."

John didn't need Zack's direction. His body was frozen in place anyway. Internally, his heart rate skyrocketed and his brain's commands to leap to his feet and run for the hills screaming were falling on deaf ears. Sweat instantly burst into drops on his forehead and his scalp and ran down his back. His throat became as parched as the desert sand in which he sat on all fours like a statue.

"Slowly move back," Zack said. "Sloooowly."

As fast as a wounded turtle, John eased his head away from the cobra. He wasn't sure he was moving at all, but he heard Zack telling him he was doing a good job.

The snake flicked out its tongue, tasting the air. The sudden movement made John want to bolt, but he held his ground and suppressed a whimper. He thought he heard Sarah gasp.

John took a careful breath and it felt like the first since he'd fallen. It didn't relax him one bit.

Then the cobra started dancing. Wait, *dancing*? John couldn't help but shake his head a tiny bit, blinking, as if he was imagining it. The gesture made the snake stop his bobbing and focus again on John, flicking its tongue out.

"Don't move," Zack said. "I've got him now."

The snake started dancing again, bobbing its head back and forth like it had invisible headphones pumping music into its tiny ear holes.

"It just can't fight the feeling," Sarah said. "Got dance fever." She snapped her fingers in rhythm with the snake's moves.

Carefully tilting his head only a few millimeters,

John could see that Zack held a necklace at arm's length. Swinging it back and forth in a rhythmic movement, the dark green of the necklace's stone pendant caught the glint of the sun, and the snake followed it back and forth, back and forth.

With the cobra hypnotized, Zack stepped away from John. The snake followed.

"Okay, carefully and quietly move away, John," Zack commanded.

John followed the order and with extreme caution pushed himself up onto his feet and stepped away to a safe distance. When he was clear, Zack backed away from the snake too, then scooped the necklace behind his body to hide it from the cobra.

The cobra stopped dancing. John could have sworn it looked confused for a few seconds before it deflated its flared hood and shrunk back down to the ground.

The kids watched it slither away.

"Oh, man, that was close." John felt a sudden wave of relief and exhaustion. His legs began to shake, and he leaned over with his hands on his knees.

"That was awesome!" Sarah said, patting John

on the back repeatedly. "You were so cool under pressure, John. Nice work."

John could feel his heart pounding in his chest, but he had to admit it felt more like exhilaration than fear at this point. Maybe the excitement of having confronted extreme danger—even death!—to live to tell about it. He stood up and took a huge breath and shouted, "Woo-hoo! I don't want to do that again."

Zack and Sarah burst out laughing.

"You were amazing, Zack," Sarah said.

"Dude, thank you," John said, holding up his hand.

Zack just looked at the upheld palm.

"Slap it," John said, shaking his hand. "It's a high five."

Zack smacked John's palm with his own.

"That's it!" John said, laughing.

Zack gave the high five another good slap. Then another. "Woo!"

"Woo-hoo!" John screamed, caught up in the moment.

The next high-five attempt missed, and Zack thwacked John on the head, which sent them both into uncontrollable laughter. John fell to the sand as if he'd been hurt, laughing the whole way down.

Sarah rolled her eyes.

When John calmed down after a couple minutes, his cheeks hurt from laughing so hard. He took a big breath and then reached out to accept Zack's extended hand.

"That was very cool," John said, hoisting himself back onto his feet. "I mean, never again. But . . ."

"I don't like snakes, but that *was* cool," Sarah said.

"You don't like cobras?" Zack asked in surprise.

Sarah yanked her chin down and shot Zack a look. "As if anyone likes venomous reptiles?"

Zack snorted from his nose and shook his head. "Call-oh-raw-doe must be such a strange place. Do you not have rats there?"

"Uh, sure, we have rats," John said, still breathing heavy and feeling giddy.

"How do you control them without cobras?" Zack said. "They keep our grain stores free from rodents. They represent our goddess Wadjet, the protector. The cobra symbol is worn on the crown of the king. She's the daughter of Ra."

"I like the idea of a goddess protector," Sarah said.

"You'll see many carvings of Wadjet in the pyramid," Zack said, "along with the eye of Ra. So King Djoser will be protected in the afterlife."

"The eye of Ra," John mused. Something about that image sounded familiar.

Zack tied the necklace's leather strap around his neck, then held up the dark green pendant, a finely carved gemstone. "The eye of Ra saved you from that cobra."

Sarah looked closely at the symbol, holding it in her palm. The pink that flushed Zack's cheeks made John wonder if Zack felt embarrassed by Sarah's proximity or liked it. Or both.

"I've seen this," Sarah said, looking at John with her eyes wide. "In the cave. Remember, John?"

The pendant was shaped like an eye with a brow, and a line that flowed down into a curlicue end, and another line pointing straight down with a knifelike edge.

Suddenly it clicked. "That's right!" John said,

recalling again the bright flash of light. "You were tracing the eye of Ra with your finger. Then there was a—"

"Bright light," Sarah finished his sentence. "Could this be a clue?"

"A clue to what?" Zack asked, pulling the necklace away from Sarah's palm and tucking it back into his tunic.

Both John and Sarah opened their mouths, but nothing came out. How could they possibly explain what had happened to them?

When they arrived at the pyramid, two other similar-aged kids came running over—a thick boy with hair to his shoulders and a short girl with a bob cut. Zack introduced them. "John and Sarah, this is Netjerichet and Ellasandra, my friends. Guys, John and Sarah are new here. They're from across the Great Green Sea, so take it easy on them for their first day, okay?"

Sarah stuck out a hand. John shied behind his more exuberant sister when meeting new people.

"Happy to meet you," she said, in all honesty. "Mind if we call you Rich and Ella?"

Ella looked at Zack and laughed, as if Zack had brought a strange pet for show-and-tell.

"Sure," Rich said, looking strangely at Sarah's extended hand. "Do you want something?"

"You shake it," Sarah said.

"Shake it?" Ella said with a subtle sneer. She was smaller than all of them, but John had the impression she could wrestle with the best. It seemed Rich was her older brother and since he looked so strong, she would have to be tough to keep up. They both had light brown skin, pale blue eyes, and sandy brown hair from which he could smell a rich lavender across the distance.

"Here, watch." Sarah turned to John. "Nice to meet you, sir."

John rolled his eyes, embarrassed by his sister's silly demonstration, but he clapped his palm in hers and let her shake it.

"Odd," Rich said.

"Odd," Ella repeated.

"We never actually do this," John said.

Sarah grimaced at her brother. "Adults do, so

we should too." Turning to Rich, she added, "Try it."

Rich turned to Ella and stuck out his hand. "Nice to meet you, sir."

John laughed and Ella turned to him with a scowl.

"You've got it," Sarah said, grasping their hands in hers and pumping it up and down.

"Why do you do it?" Zack asked.

Sarah shrugged. "I dunno. It's just what we do, I guess."

John didn't know either, but he made a mental note to research the origin of the handshake when he got back home.

"Ready to help out with this beautiful pyramid?" Zack asked.

"Ready!" Sarah exclaimed, jumping up into the air.

"I guess," John said. "What're we doing?"

"Well, as we talked about last night, I'm a scribe, so I write down the legends," Zack said. "But you can do whatever you want."

"What's it like being a scribe?" John asked. "Sounds easy."

"It's slow and careful work. And you're in the dark with only a lamp for most of the day."

"I like to work with the rolling team," Ella said.

"What do they do?" Sarah asked.

Ella pointed to laborers handling stone slabs with thick corded ropes. The giant blocks seemed to levitate across the sand.

"How are they doing that?" John wanted to know.

"Rollers," Ella said.

Rich filled in: "We put boards down on the sand, then round logs on the boards. Once we have the piece of rock on the logs, we can just roll it across the desert to the hoisting team." He pointed to scaffolding with a group of men working a system of ramps with ropes and pulleys.

"Where does the rock come from?" John asked. Besides a few scattered rocks and boulders, they were surrounded by barren desert.

"Oh," Rich said, "you can't see it from here, but there's a trench on the other side, a quarry where we get the stone. We've dug down deep enough to the bedrock for the limestone. We polish the finest pieces for the outer walls and to line the tunnels inside."

"Ah, like the ones at your house," John said to Zack.

"Right." Zack nodded.

Rich pursed his lips. Was that jealousy?

"And we're almost done," Ella said, barely containing her excitement.

"That's right," Rich said. "Only a few more weeks until the solstice and our pyramid is complete. Your father must be pretty happy, Zachariah. About your move."

Zack smiled, but John could tell a fake when he saw one. John was the master of fake smiles, after all. John remembered back to dinner the previous night, when discussion of the move had elicited Zack's groans.

Ella tugged on Rich's tunic. "Come on, Netjerichet. You know how he feels about that." Based on Rich's clenched jaw, John thought that Rich knew exactly what he was doing by provoking Zack about the move. Rich was Zack's friend?

"Right. Sorry," Rich said, turning his eyes to the sand.

"It's okay," Zack said. "I just wish I could stay

here."

"Is there any way you could?" Rich asked, seeming genuine. Maybe Rich had acted the way he had a moment ago because he was angry Zack was leaving. Could that be? Could he be showing his frustration that he was losing a friend? It made John wonder how Roman felt about his move to Maryland. John realized he'd never asked Roman how he felt about it.

With a glare that said *knock it off*, Ella kicked Rich's foot.

"Not unless something happened to the construction, I guess," Zack said. "But my father's so precise that it's hard to imagine that happening."

"You never know," Rich said, "there could be bad weather. Or an accident. Or—"

"Anyway," Ella interrupted. "I'm gonna get to work. Do you want to come with me, Sarah?"

"I'd love to," Sarah replied. They walked off together, and Sarah spun around. "Meet you for lunch?"

"Yeah," John and Zack said at the same time.

"Do you want to work with me in the tunnels?" Zack asked John.

"Maybe," John said. "What d'you do, Rich?"

Rich flexed his bicep. The muscles in his forearm tightened under the skin. "I like to work the heavy stuff. Hoist team for me."

Working in the dark, or working with heavy stone slabs. John didn't like the idea of going down into a spooky tunnel in the middle of a pyramid, but it sounded cushier than hoisting duty.

"I'm with you," John said, slapping his new buddy Zack on the shoulder. Half realizing it, John had just labeled Zack a friend.

"All right," Zack said. "Let's go get tied up and get some oil lamps."

"Tied up?" John asked.

"Just a precaution, in case our lamps go out and we're stranded in the dark, then we can't lose each other."

Stranded in the dark? Lose each other? Maybe he should have decided on hoisting duty.

John held up the dim oil lamp and descended into

the pitch-black tunnel. A thick rope tied around his waist secured him to Zack ahead. The steep slant of the passageway was slippery with grit and sand. His hand against the wall, John placed one foot in front of the other and tried not to think about how far they'd gone away from the light, from the outside. Surprisingly, John could feel a subtle breeze.

"Do I feel wind?" he asked.

"There are small vent shafts that lead to the outside. So King Djoser's ka can smell the Nile," Zack said. John took a whiff of the air but could smell only dirt.

John had his head down, watching his feet shuffle on the descending path. When he looked up, he gasped and stopped.

"Isn't it magnificent?" Zack said, shining his lamp to the wall.

The light danced over beautiful artwork and intricate designs, paintings and crisp engraved forms that were more alive and pristine than in any school textbook John had ever seen. He wished he had a phone to take pictures of the captivating art. They showed people tilling the land, crops growing in the water, eagles and cows and kings and on and on. It nearly made him forget that they were underneath a zillion tons of heavy rock in a tiny rectangular tunnel, heading deeper into the cramped earth.

When Zack turned around to move on, John nearly dropped his lamp. He jumped back, which tugged on the rope and pulled Zack along with him. Zack let out an "*oof!*"

"Spi-spi-spi—" John couldn't spit out the word, pointing at Zack's back. A group of large hairy spiders as black as a moonless night twitched and hung by their spindly legs from Zack's tunic.

Zack turned around. "What is it?"

"Spiders," John squeaked.

Zack spun so rapidly that his flame sputtered. "Where?"

"On your back!"

With his only free hand, Zack swatted at his back in a goofy way while spinning around and around, which shortened the rope between them, moving him closer to John.

John backed up, but that tugged Zack—and the spiders!—right along with him. There was no escaping them!

Swinging his lamp at the creatures, John set one on fire and it leapt to the floor. It skittered into the darkness, lighting the path with its trailing flame.

"Careful!" Zack exclaimed.

John used his hand and batted at another spider hitchhiking a ride on Zack's back. It went flying into the wall, then chased off down the passage. The creatures, as big as a fist, felt like hairy tennis balls.

Both boys hopped around, the enormous spiders scurrying away from their stomping feet. Once they had all disappeared, John stood panting, smiling, amazed that he'd had the courage to swipe at those huge spiders.

"Okay, that was freaky," John said.

"More than the cobra?" Zack asked, catching his breath too. He held his palm up for a high five.

"Uhhh, maybe." John landed the high five. "No. Cobra wins." They both laughed.

Zack turned and kept moving. John wasn't sure he wanted to follow Zack down into the dark tunnel anymore, and especially down the same direction the spiders had fled, but the rope tugged at his waist, nudging his feet into forward steps. Instead of admiring the artwork on the walls, John scanned for more creatures.

John watched Zack ahead of him. Now that he and Zack had fought off a cobra and spiders together, he did feel—

"There's all sorts of things living down here. Bats, for example. They like the cool darkness," Zack said. "And of course in the burial chamber itself we keep many symbols of Serket, the goddess who protects the dead."

"Protects the dead?" John asked, his mind conjuring hideous mythical beasts.

"Scorpions have a deadly stinger, though," Zack added. "So stay clear of them."

"Scorpions?" John asked, his voice cracking. "You keep scorpions down here?"

"Of course," Zack answered. "Like I said, scorpions represent Serket, our goddess who protects the dead. She also represents nature and animals and medicine and magic and—"

"Wow, she does it all," John interrupted. "Magic, you said?"

"Serket—the scorpion—has magic, yes."

"Well, regardless, I don't think I need to see any of those today," John said, giving a slight shudder. "I've had enough of the heebie-jeebies for one day."

Zack pointed to a side passage. They turned the corner and went down further. John was wondering how much more they had to go when Zack abruptly stopped and said, "Here we are. Something I made. I wanted to show you."

John held up his lamp to illuminate a series of hieroglyphs precisely carved into the limestone wall. "What is it?"

Zack smiled, obviously proud of his work. "It tells the story of Ra traveling across space and time. His chariot, pulled by beams of light, carries the ka of King Djoser to wherever he wants to go, and grants him understanding of all languages past and present and future."

"Across space and time," John repeated, holding the lamp closer to the art.

"Pretty great, right?" Zack asked, his eyes aglow.

John laughed. "Yeah, it's exactly what we've been looking for."

His lamp hovered near a carving of the eye of Ra.

"And it's repeated here." Zack shone his light on the opposite wall. "And here." He cast his light on another set of hieroglyphs, which included the eye of Ra. "And many more throughout the pyramid."

The electric thrill of discovery that had surged through John when he first saw the carved eye of Ra faded as quickly as a static shock when he realized the symbol was repeated probably hundreds of times—thousands?—throughout the pyramid. Regardless, one of these had to be the key. Right?

CHAPTER SIX

Growing Storm

SARAH

Sarah thought she heard her name over the steady groan of the limestone slabs rolling across the logs. The boards under the logs creaked, grinding the sand below with tons of pressure. Sarah's job—to ensure that the ends of each block lined up with the edge of the boards so they didn't get off course —meant she spent most of the time with her eyes down. When she looked up, she saw Ella pulling out one of the logs from the back and hoisting it onto her shoulder. As the stone progressed down the track, the logs at the end were moved to the front of the line, so they were constantly moving the stone on the same set of logs. This way, they could traverse any distance with a small number of logs and boards. Enough to fit on only two mules, plus an additional mule to carry some water and various supplies. Ella hummed to herself while she worked. Sarah had never heard the tune before, but the way it jumped up and down, the musical scale sounded peculiar to Sarah. Catchy, just different.

Sarah caught herself staring at Ella, thinking about the song, when one of the other laborers on the rolling team—a young man maybe twenty years old named Aten with curious green eyes— shouted something at Sarah. It snapped her attention back to her work, and she could see the stone's edge was no longer parallel with the board beneath it. Uh-oh. Her side was in need of course correction. She put her shoulder into it, and as the mules moved it forward another foot, she pushed it back on track going straight.

When Ella had first told her what she would be doing—moving a massive limestone block with only her body's strength—she laughed out loud thinking it a practical joke. But after the demonstration by Aten and Ella, she jumped in and gave it a try. She was surprised by how easily the rectangular stone shifted while it moved under the rolling pins. Her mind flashed to the table at the security line in the airport, the one you put your suitcase on to feed it into the scanning machine. It consisted of a bunch of steel rolling pins, and moving even a heavy suitcase could be done with minimal effort.

Once her block was back on track, she swore she heard her name again, but this time it was closer. She spun around. Rich was approaching, about fifty yards away and waving both arms.

"Hey, Rich!" She waved at him.

Aten, the laborer on the opposite corner of her block, shouted at her to pay attention.

Sarah flinched and scanned her lines. "Even Steven, as parallel as a good downhill skier's tips." She rolled her eyes at Aten.

Rich was closer now, shouting. "We have to go. Now! Danger."

The people all stopped, but the mules kept going.

"Danger?" Sarah asked.

"Look." Rich pointed with a stiff arm to the horizon as if he were trying to reach out and touch the distant line where earth met sky.

The rolling team all turned in unison to match Rich's gaze. The block rolled askew and slipped a corner off its log, embedding itself in the sand. Aten cursed in frustration, but ignored the blunder when he saw the danger that Rich was pointing at.

"What am I looking for?" Sarah said. The other rolling team members, including Ella, immediately started untying the mules.

"What's happening?" Sarah asked.

"Come with me," Rich said. "We need to get to shelter as fast as we can." He grabbed Sarah by the elbow, but she stood her ground and twisted out of his grasp. Rich stumbled to a stop and looked back at her.

"Tell me what's going on!" she demanded, stomping her foot.

Rich came back to her. Standing by her side, he pointed again, his eyes still to the horizon. Sarah squinted and could see a fine brushstroke of dark clouds against the bright blue canvas of the sky. It stretched from one end of the line to the other, as far as she could see.

"Thunderstorm?" Sarah didn't understand what was so scary about some distant rain clouds.

Rich scoffed. "Much worse."

"What, then?"

"Sandstorm," Rich said, in the gravest of tones.

"Why is that such a big deal?" Sarah asked. She had never experienced a sandstorm before, but she found it unbelievable that these people were so afraid of a little sandy wind.

"Trust me, you don't want to be caught in a sandstorm," Rich said. "The wind is so fierce, whipping the sand around so fast, it can strip an animal carcass down to the bones in a minute."

That sent a shiver through Sarah's skeleton and her skin suddenly became cold. "Okay, you convinced me."

Ella tugged on the rope that led a mule behind her. "Let's go. There's no time to waste."

They started off back toward the village. Sarah only took a few steps before she stopped in her tracks. "What about John and Zack? Are they safe in the pyramid?"

"Probably," Ella said.

"*Probably?*" Sarah blurted.

"Well," Ella said, "since the tunnels run down, if the entrance isn't sealed and the storm is big enough, it could fill in and block the passage."

"What?!" Sarah's eyes went wide.

"It's okay," Rich said. "We can dig them out tomorrow."

"If it's even that bad of a storm," Ella said, shrugging.

"No way!" Sarah shouted, shaking her head. "We have to warn them!"

"Sarah, we have to get to shelter," Rich said, pulling her by the elbow again. "They'll be fine. Come on."

Sarah hesitated in her steps, turned her head back, and stared at the pyramid. Rich and Ella seemed confident that John would be okay but . . . The artist's brushstroke of darkness had grown from a fine line into the smear made by a full-size house painter's tool. It had grown so quickly, and she could now see it moving toward them. Sarah held her breath.

John.

Sarah yanked her elbow out of Rich's grasp and took off running toward the pyramid, sand kicking up from her heels.

"Sarah!" Rich yelled after her, but she didn't slow down. She pumped her legs, head down, her whole body pushing to go faster.

When Sarah neared the tunnel, she took a breath and started yelling. "John! Zack!"

No response.

A second later: "Zack!" It was Ella who'd screamed this time. Sarah jumped in surprise. She hadn't heard Ella following her in the sand.

"You're fast for being so small," Sarah muttered.

Ella narrowed her eyes, seemingly insulted by Sarah's comment.

"Zack! John!" It was Rich's turn to shout for their friends, surprising Sarah again.

"You guys—came?" Sarah stammered with a half smile, both shocked and happy they hadn't left her—or her brother—alone. But the moment was fleeting.

No one was answering their calls. The dark tunnel leading into the pyramid yawned like a tired cat, a dark hole that looked menacing, as if the jagged edges of the doorway were pointed teeth ready to spear them as a saber-tooth tiger would.

Sarah plunged in headfirst. As soon as she was inside, she flashed back to the cave that had brought them here. It was so quiet and so, so dark. She had the vague sense that there was light behind her, and knew in her brain that Rich and Ella were there too, yet it felt like she'd fallen into a pit and was still falling down the sloped tunnel.

"John!" she screamed with all her guts. "Zack!" Then she stood still, listening.

"Sarah?" came a response. It was John!

"John!" Sarah jumped with excitement, and her skull smacked against the low roof of the small tunnel. It sent her clobbering to the ground, clutching her head.

"Are you all right?" Ella knelt down to Sarah.

Rich continued, "Zack! Sandstorm. Let's go!"

"I'm okay," Sarah said, standing up, rubbing her head. "John?"

A pinprick of light appeared down the hallway, hovering and wavering like a spirit from beyond. As it neared, it jostled up and down and sputtered with rapid movement. Soon, the shapes of John and Zack running emerged from the darkness.

Sarah held her head while smiling at her little brother. He smiled back, showing the lone dimple on his right cheek.

Everyone stared at each other for a moment before Rich broke the silence. "See, maybe weather *will* delay the construction and you won't have to move," he said, trying to lighten the mood. "Imhotep can't control that!"

Zack frowned, clearly not amused. "Ha, only a couple hours at best. If we survive it."

That shriveled any attempt at mood lightening.

"On that cheery note, let's get outta here," Ella said.

When all five of them got back outside, the wall of the dark storm stretched high into the sky, blotting out the sun. Though it was midday, it looked more like dusk. The wind howled and shrieked like a banshee, warning of impending doom. As they moved toward the village, pushing on with their shirts over their mouths and noses, sand levitated from the ground in front of them and got sucked into their faces. It stung their cheeks and bit into their eyes. Sarah shielded her view with her hand and pushed on, but their progress felt slower than the pace of the storm gaining on them.

"We're not going to make it!" Sarah yelled over the deafening storm.

"What?" John yelled back.

"We're not—going—to make it!" she shouted again, more deliberate with her words.

"Come on," Ella said, nudging them along. "We have to keep moving!"

Rich tugged at John's arm, moving him forward. Zack led the way. Though he was close in front of Sarah, she could barely see his silhouette amid the swirling sand.

Then, in a blink, Zack disappeared. Sarah stopped.

"Don't stop!" John pleaded.

Where Zack had disappeared, Sarah could still see Ella in the front, followed by Rich, then John and Sarah. Ella turned and looked back. Sarah could tell Ella was shouting something to her, but couldn't make out the words through the raging chaos of the storm.

Then as quickly as Zack had disappeared, Ella

did too. Had they been sucked up into the sky? Or swallowed down into the sandy earth below?

Sarah could feel panic vibrating in her temples. Her breathing was choked with sand, and her nose ran with snot. She didn't want to inhale any more grit. She didn't want to breathe in any more sand. If she never saw another grain of sand in her life, that would be okay. She gripped her brother by the hand and squeezed.

John squeezed back.

Suddenly Rich grabbed Sarah by the wrist. She looked up at him through the slits in her fingers. Sarah could see that Rich had his other arm extended in the opposite direction. The view wavered clear enough for a moment that she saw a chain of them holding hands. John held on to Sarah. Sarah held on to Rich. And farther down, Rich held on to Ella. At the head of the train, Ella held on to Zack's hand. And Zack was waving. The curtain of sand enveloped them again and she lost sight of everyone but Rich, his other hand extending into a cloud of buzzing dirt.

Sarah couldn't speak. She pulled John close and hugged him tight. He buried his head in her embrace and they stood like that, Sarah holding on to Rich's hand with all her might.

A sudden gust of even stronger wind blasted into them and sent them all tumbling to the ground, tearing Rich's grasp from Sarah's. Sarah pulled both of her arms tight around John and they rolled onto the ground together.

"I've got you!" Sarah said to her brother. She didn't know if he could hear her, but he hugged tighter. "And I know you've got me," she said.

A booming voice seemed to come from the very storm itself. Sarah saw a ghost, entirely in white, the size of a full-grown adult, leaning into the wind. He glided closer to them and his voice boomed again, seeming to come from everywhere at once.

"Hold on!" it said. The ghost bent down to them. Sarah didn't fight when the ghost picked her and John up and they floated off into the storm.

Sarah buried her head into the ghost's shoulder. She knew it was a man, but believing it was a ghost seemed easier than a person braving this wild storm and surviving. The storm seemed supernatural, so why not a ghost to save them?

CHAPTER SEVEN

It's All Fun and Games

SARAH

Zack slammed the door shut and the man set Sarah and John down on a plush rug of fluffy wool in front of a fireplace. They coughed in unison. Sarah didn't know if she'd ever not cough again. No matter how hard she hacked, she didn't think she'd ever get the grit out of her lungs.

The man unwrapped the scarf from around his head. Imhotep.

Hatmehit came in with clay mugs of herbs. She took a kettle from its hook hanging over the fire, poured steaming water into the cups, and handed one to each of the children and her husband.

"Drink," Hatmehit said.

"What is it?" John asked, sniffing the tea.

"Licorice, which is an expectorant to help you cough, and crushed garlic, to give you vitality and strength," Hatmehit said.

Sarah leaned over the rim of the mug and inhaled a whiff. Her nose hairs curled in on themselves from the strong odor and she pulled her head back, coughing to cover up the retreat and not seem rude.

Hatmehit chuckled. "It may be an odd combination, but you should drink, child. It's good for you, I promise."

John put the cup to his lips and, after testing its heat level, took several gulps. "It's not bad," he said. "The licorice flavor is dark and rich, then you have the spicy zing of the garlic. I think you may be onto something here, Mrs. . . ." He still didn't know what to call her.

"Just Hatmehit is fine, John." She smiled at him.

John finished his drink and held it out for more water, which Hatmehit was happy to oblige.

"Unfortunate we lost a half day of work,"

Imhotep grumbled. "But I'm glad you're safe." He put his hand on the back of Zack's neck and looked him in the eye. "You were very brave and quick thinking out there to latch hands with your friends. I may not have found them if you hadn't created that chain."

"A chain of friends," John said, glancing at Zack. He rubbed his hands together in front of the fire.

"Yeah, thanks, Zack," Sarah added.

"This is quite a storm too," Imhotep said. "I imagine we'll need to spend some time tomorrow digging out the passages. Good thing you decided not to stay in the pyramid."

"Thank Sarah," Zack said, looking over to Sarah.

Sarah smiled. "It was definitely a team effort."

Imhotep bowed his head. "Yes. But thank you, Sarah."

"Sorry about the lost work time, Father." Zack looked at the floor.

"That's okay," Imhotep said. "We account, somewhat, for weather delays in our project planning. Tomorrow should be a big day!"

They sat together in silence for a few moments.

Sarah coughed again, but it was a mere sputter,

nothing like the harsh barking she'd been doing when they first found refuge in the house.

"The tea is working," Hatmehit said, grinning.

"You know how to work magic, my dear," Imhotep said, kissing his wife on the forehead. "Well, if we have the rest of the day off and we can't go outside, shall we play some Senet?"

"Senet?" John asked.

"It's fun. A board game," Zack said. "Do you have board games where you're from?"

"I usually win at chess," Sarah said.

"Monopoly," John said, "is more my game."

"Never heard of those," Imhotep said. "You'll have to teach us before you leave."

"Why don't we try Senet first," Sarah said.

"Before we leave?" John asked.

"Well, you don't plan on staying here forever, do you?" Imhotep replied.

"Dear," Hatmehit interjected, shooting her eyes at her husband. "We can talk about that later. Let's just enjoy some games together for now."

Sarah exchanged a glance with John. Would they have to find another place to stay here in Saqqara if they couldn't find their way back to

Colorado? How were orphans treated in ancient Egypt? Sarah hoped she wouldn't have to find out.

"Of course," Imhotep said. "Let's play Senet!"

"Wonderful," Hatmehit said. She took two boards out of a trunk and set them on the floor.

Zack crossed his legs and started rattling through the rules as he shook the dice in his fist. Sarah could tell he was excited to play. Her own excitement had dulled, thinking instead about how long until they might be asked to leave. Of course it made sense; she couldn't expect these strangers to simply take care of them forever, right?

"You roll the dice and then move these sticks around the board until you get here where you can remove them," Zack explained.

Remove them, Sarah thought, tapping her fingers on the mug.

"Looks like cribbage," John said.

"And the key," Zack continued, "is that you want to move your pieces in a way that also prevents your opponent from making his way around the board."

"So, not like cribbage," John said, smiling.

"It's only a two-person game and there are five of us," Hatmehit said, "but we do have two boards. So one person will get to watch each round."

"Let's begin!" Imhotep exclaimed, clapping his hands together, seeming almost as giddy as his son at the prospect of the entertainment.

Zack challenged John, and Hatmehit went up against her husband. Sarah observed, though she wasn't really paying attention to the game. Maybe if she helped around the house and was super polite, maybe Hatmehit would keep them a little longer. Maybe—

A few moves in, Zack let out a cheer and pumped his fist in the air.

Sarah thought back to their own family game nights. "Some things never change, even after thousands of years. Right, John?"

John chuckled and nodded.

Hatmehit laughed at something Imhotep had said, and watching her throw her head back in joy gave Sarah a warm feeling in her chest. She thought more about her own mother and father and their home. Playing board games as a family in front of the fireplace on a snowy winter night, laughing and being together with hot mugs of cocoa.

After several rounds of intense competition and good-natured fun, the games went back into the trunk. Hatmehit and Imhotep went into the kitchen to prepare dinner. Sarah could hear them talking and wondered if she and John were the subject of their discussion.

The storm still raged outside, shaking the house from time to time. Even if they got kicked out tomorrow, for now Sarah knew they were safe. She felt it in her gut.

Zack went into the kitchen to help his parents, leaving Sarah and John alone.

Sarah sat next to her brother, and they both stared into the fire, watched its tendrils flick around like a cobra's tongue.

"I miss Mom and Dad," she said.

John sighed. "Me too."

"Remember when we were little and you got the boot from Monopoly stuck in your nose?"

John said, "Ugh, don't remind me."

"And Dad was trying to fish it out with tweezers, and Mom was laughing so hard, which made me laugh, which made you laugh, and Dad was getting frustrated at you laughing while he was trying to do delicate nasal surgery on you, but it just made Mom laugh harder, which made me laugh harder—"

"And the boot shot right out of my nose—"

"Which made Dad crack up. And we're all laughing so hard—I mean, tears streaming down our cheeks. And Dad picks you up and smothers you with kisses and rolls you onto the floor. And me and Mom pig-pile on top . . ." Sarah gazed into the fire and back in time, reliving that joyful moment with her family.

"Oh, man, that was so fun." John's eyes were moist. "Guess it doesn't matter where we are—"

"Or *when*," Sarah said, grinning and putting her arm around her brother.

"Yeah," John said. "Or when. We have a good time, don't we? I mean, our family."

"Yeah," Sarah said.

They sat in a comfortable silence, together.

After a delicious meal of baked white fish, stewed carrots, and mashed lentils with butter, Sarah excused herself and went straight to bed. Even though it had been interrupted and cut short by the sandstorm, her first day working on the pyramids had been exhausting. None of her chores at home even came close!

John followed her lead and nestled into his own soft sheets.

"Good night, John." Sarah tousled John's hair. Surprisingly, John didn't resist like he usually did.

"Night, sis," John said, yawning. "Tomorrow's a big day."

Sarah gave a tired grin, recognizing Imhotep's nightly proclamation.

A few moments passed. Sarah listened to the chirping insects outside and thought about home and the sounds of the forest. This place in ancient Egypt felt so far away, and yet not that different at the same time. A warm home, full belly, and the feeling of safety. Sarah smiled at the comfortable feeling, but with a tear in her eye. No matter how welcoming Zack's family had been, they still weren't *her* family. And who knew when she'd see them again?

"John, you awake?"

She could hear his deep, rhythmic breathing.

Sarah's eyes burned with fatigue and her bones relished the stillness of lying down, but her mind raced like a hummingbird. A barrage of thoughts came one after the other: thinking about where they'd go if Imhotep kicked them out; wondering what her friends—Cynthia and Maxine—were doing; remembering the ominous darkness of the sandstorm; how Rich and Ella had followed her to the pyramid to save John and Zack; the old fort she and John made in the woods, the one they'd gone off trail to investigate; how she'd barged right into the dark cave without thinking about it twice, despite John's pleas.

Sarah's eyes opened, dismissing the mental movie reel. This was all her fault. They wouldn't be stuck in ancient Egypt if she hadn't charged into that hole in the ground without thinking about the impacts of the decision. She hadn't considered what might happen, and how that might affect people like John. Sarah thought of her parents, probably worried sick, and it made her stomach flip-flop. If only she'd stayed on the hiking trail, her parents might be giving her a good-night kiss right now.

John mumbled something in his sleep and turned over.

Sarah heard footsteps outside their door. All the lamps in the house had been blown out, so whoever it was moved through the dark of night.

Sarah imagined it was Hatmehit. A warm hug from the woman sounded like something Sarah could use right now. She wouldn't say it out loud being a seventh grader, after all—but maybe she'd just check if Hatmehit was up.

Stepping carefully around John, Sarah went to the threshold of the doorway. She paused, then almost turned and went back to bed. But something tugged at her to go out and talk with Hatmehit. Sarah knew she wouldn't be able to get to sleep until she tried. Just one hug, no big deal.

Leaning out of her bedroom, she saw a silhouette at the front door. With one hand on the doorknob, when he turned his head to scan the room, Sarah saw it was Zack. She wasn't sure why she did it, but she ducked back to avoid him seeing her. When she peeked out again, Zack pulled a dark hood over his head and stepped out of the house. The storm still spit a little, but it had all but died.

Where was he going?

Sarah had never snuck out of her own house, but given how stealthy he'd acted, it didn't seem like this was Zack's first time. She listened for a moment longer, holding her breath: only the sound of the chirping insects. Everyone else in the house slept.

Sarah crept back to her bed and pulled up the fine linen sheet to her chin. Her eyes were wide, staring up at the ceiling. Did she really know Zack that well? What was he doing that he had to sneak around in the middle of the night?

For the first time since they arrived in ancient Egypt, even accounting for the trial of being lost in the sandstorm, Sarah felt nervous. She wanted Mom. No, not nervous—she felt scared.

Scared and alone.

Sarah worries about
Ricked Out

CHAPTER EIGHT

Sabotage

SARAH

"No!" The voice boomed through the house.

"Wha—?" The single word jolted Sarah awake. She scratched her groggy head, felt the tangles of red hair from a short and fitful sleep. "Am I late for school? I'm getting up." She tossed the sheets aside.

Sarah swung her legs to the floor. The touch of brick on her bare feet—instead of carpeting—reminded her that she wasn't home in Colorado.

John's bed was empty.

"Find the thief!" shouted the man in the other

room.

Sarah recognized the voice of Imhotep, obviously upset. She walked out into the kitchen and saw Zack and John sitting quiet at the table, eating a breakfast of bread slathered with a dark-colored chunky jam. Hatmehit leaned back in her chair with a steaming mug of herbs, a look of empathy arching her eyebrows as she watched her husband pacing the room.

Imhotep put his hand on his forehead. Near him stood Aten, the rolling-team laborer who had been the taskmaster nagging at Sarah on her first day. Aten was only as tall as Zack, shorter than John, and certainly shorter than Imhotep. So when Imhotep glared down at Aten, Aten cowered.

"I'm sorry, sir," Aten said, looking up with his distinct green eyes. "They must have used the cover of the sandstorm. The damage is—"

"I know," Imhotep said. "This is going to waylay our plans." He clenched his fist. "We're going to miss our target date."

"Can't we just deliver the pyramid on the deadline and assure the king that the damage will be repaired?" Aten rubbed his hands together nervously.

Imhotep pointed a finger at Aten. "I want who-ever did this caught. Let everyone in Saqqara know there will be a reward for the thief's head." Imhotep snapped his hand across his neck, pre-tending to chop off his own head.

Hatmehit sighed and looked out the window. A flock of brown-and-white birds flew by.

"What?" Imhotep asked her. "You don't think the punishment fits the crime?"

"Darling." Hatmehit set down her tea. "You know I prefer to err on the side of due process and reform instead of just going around lopping off anyone's head who has ever done something wrong."

Imhotep clenched his jaw, breathed in and out, and looked at the ceiling.

"But," she continued, "I know that you and King Djoser will act in the best interest of Saqqara and our community. What did the thief steal?"

"The head of a statue," Aten said, "of Wadjet."

"A head for a head," Imhotep said, fuming.

Sarah remembered that Wadjet was a goddess that protected the people, especially the king, represented by a cobra. She'd seen a few statues and carvings, usually of a woman with the head of a cobra, its hood flared and fangs out.

"How big was it?" Hatmehit asked.

"It was a lifelike statue in the burial chamber, so as big as yours or mine," Aten answered.

"I don't understand why would anyone steal the head of Wadjet," Hatmehit said. "It doesn't make sense."

"Especially if they knew they'd be risking their own head," Aten added.

"Who knows why thieves do what they do? Regardless, they'll suffer the consequences," Imhotep said, smacking his fist into his open palm.

"So," Zack spoke up, his voice timid, "how long does this delay the project?"

Sarah flashed back to last night, when Zack had thrown the hood over his head and snuck out of the house. He had motive to delay the project—he didn't want to move. Had he been the saboteur? He wouldn't do that to his father. Would he?

"A week, maybe two," Aten answered.

"Not if I can help it," Imhotep said.

"Sir, we have to acquire the stone, the artists

need to sculpt it, then we have to hoist it up into the chamber where it was removed, and—" Aten put out his hands palms up in a gesture like *There's nothing I can do.*

"I want double shifts. Recruit more laborers if you have to. We'll pay overtime too."

Aten licked his lips, but he didn't say a word. The idea of extra pay seemed to have struck a nerve.

"We *will* hit our target date, Aten. Now go, there's work to be done." Imhotep waved him off.

"As you wish," Aten said. He bowed and rushed out of the house.

"I'm sorry, children," Imhotep said. He flashed a forced smile. Sarah could tell he was trying to portray a more relaxed state. "I'm going to be working longer hours this week, it seems. Have to make sure everything is done on time for the king." He picked up a piece of bread from the cutting board and took a bite. After kissing his wife on the forehead, he picked up his mug of herbal tea and headed for the door.

With one foot outside, he turned back and looked at Zack. "I'll see you shortly?"

"But—" Zack looked to his mother.

"Zack?" Imhotep glared.

"Yes, Father," Zack said. Then when Imhotep was gone and out of earshot: "But it's so early, Mom."

"I know, dear, but your father really needs your help," Hatmehit said. "And I'm sure you'll make the responsible choice."

"Ugh, that's what you say whenever I have to do something I don't want to do," Zack groaned.

Sarah chuckled but put her hand to her mouth to hide it. John kicked her under the table.

Hatmehit grinned. "Maybe. But it's still true." She winked at Sarah.

John had seconds, which didn't seem to be a problem for their schedule, since Zack was eating like a sleepy sloth in slow motion.

"Hatmehit?" Sarah asked.

"Yes, dear?"

"Why is this target date so important to Imhotep?"

Hatmehit paused and thought about her answer. "Well, for a few reasons, I'd say. One is financial: If he hits the target date, we get a big monetary bonus. And even more than that, delivering on time would earn us favor with the king that's priceless."

John perked up. "Cash and the ear of the king. I can understand that."

"But the most important reason to my husband is respect. He planned this project for years, plotting every detail, every potential for schedule disruption. He made every decision on the materials to be used, the mechanisms to get the stone out of the ground and into the air. This is a project that has never been done before, that may stand for thousands of years."

Sarah winked at John. Little did they know that it would indeed! "I think it will."

"He cares more about that pyramid than he does his own family," Zack said.

Hatmehit continued, "At the end of the day, money comes and goes. Buildings erode into the sand. Ra sets and rises again. But your word— your honor—that is something that you have to work ceaselessly to maintain. Respect is hard won and easily lost. Remember that, Zack. That is the most important thing for your father."

Zack ate the last big hunk of his bread in one bite, suddenly not trying to stall any longer. He got up in a huff from the table, cleared his plate, and disappeared down the hallway.

John and Sarah finished their breakfasts and thanked Hatmehit.

"You're quite welcome, my dears. Your parents taught you wonderful manners."

"I hope we can go home soon," Sarah said. "But I hope we can stay here until that time comes."

"I—" Hatmehit paused and seemed to choose her words carefully. "I hope for that too." She gave a subtle smile that didn't reveal any clues to Sarah about how long they might be welcome.

"I'm going to get ready," Sarah said. "John, come with me?"

John gave her a one-eyebrow-up stare. "I'm already ready."

"Just come on," she said through closed teeth.

"Ooookay," John said, shrugging to Hatmehit.

In their bedroom, Sarah whispered, "John, I have to tell you something."

"What's going on?" John asked. The way his eyes widened and his feet shifted, Sarah could tell her comment made him worry.

"I don't know if . . . I think . . . I mean, I saw . . ."

"What, Sarah, what?" John pleaded.

"Shhh," she said to him, pulling him by the elbow farther away from the doorway. "Last night, I couldn't fall asleep . . ." She drifted off again. She didn't really see anything that would incriminate Zack, did she?

"I conked right out," John said. "But I can tell this isn't about your insomnia. Come on, sis, you can tell me. What's up?"

"Zack snuck out of the house last night." Sarah exhaled as if she'd dropped a dumbbell.

John squished one cheek up and squeezed his eyes together, staring at Sarah. "So?"

"And what happened at the pyramid . . ."

"Huh?"

"Geez, John, you can be so dense. Zack wants the project to take longer on the pyramid, right?"

"He doesn't want to move, sure."

"Right." Sarah nodded. "And there was damage on the pyramid last night that's going to delay the project by a couple weeks."

"Right." John nodded, still not quite getting it.

"And Zack snuck out last night."

Sarah could see the light bulb click on in John's brain as if she'd pulled on the metal chain.

"Ohhhhh," John said. Then he quieted himself and darted his eyes toward the hallway.

Sarah nodded a few times while John's gears turned.

"Oh," John said again, this time apparently having processed the implication. "And you heard what Imhotep said." He made the head-chopping gesture that Imhotep had made earlier.

"What should we do?" Sarah asked.

"Well," John said, putting his finger to his chin and spreading his feet in a pondering stance. "We don't actually have any evidence that he's the thief, right?"

"No."

"So how do we know he did it?"

"We don't."

John snapped his fingers. "Exactly. We don't. So, innocent until proven guilty, right?"

"That's due process for ya. Hatmehit would be proud. But what if he did? Should we tell Imhotep?"

"Or Hatmehit?" John said.

Sarah didn't like the idea of being a snitch, but harboring a fugitive—would that get her head cut off too if she knew who the thief was and didn't say anything?

"First we should get some evidence," John said. "I don't want to get him in trouble if it wasn't him."

"Yeah, maybe he was just out for a walk," Sarah said, rolling her eyes. "In the middle of the night with a hood on."

"Yeah, okay, it looks bad."

"Whatever we do," Sarah said, "we can't let Zack know."

"Know what?" Zack said, suddenly poking his head into their room.

Sarah flinched a little, but John jumped a foot off the ground and yelped like a little dog would if someone stepped on its paw.

"Whoa," Zack said. "Didn't mean to startle you."

"Yeah, yeah, just startled me, that's all," John said awkwardly, shaking his head about eight times and looking back and forth from Sarah to

Zack about five times.

"My brother can be a little skittish," Sarah said. "But he's fine. Right, bro?" Her eyes drilled into him.

"Fine, perfectly fine. Everything is coming up roses here. You?" John asked Zack.

"What were you talking about?" Zack asked John.

"What do you mean?" John said.

Sarah stepped in to save her stammering brother. "Don't worry about it. We were planning a little surprise for you. To thank you. Too bad you found out. But don't ruin it more, will you?" She walked past him out the door and slugged him on the shoulder in a playful way.

"What is it?" Zack asked.

"Well, if we told you, it wouldn't be a surprise, now would it, silly?" Sarah said. "Don't we need to get to work?"

"Hi ho, hi ho, it's off to work we go!" John sang. He followed his sister toward the door.

"You guys want to stay on the same teams as yesterday? Or switch it up?" Zack asked as they walked down the hallway together.

"I think I want to work with you two today," Sarah said. She could see John's relief in how he relaxed his shoulders. Zack was a nice kid; there's no way he'd do anything to harm her little brother. But Sarah knew that sometimes when people lied, they felt obligated to continue with the lie to avoid a shameful confession. And sometimes, when someone keeps a lie going like that, the lie and the shame both grow and become more complicated, and more lies are stacked on top of it, compounding the shame, until it becomes a huge double-decker cheeseburger of dishonesty and regret. And when someone is stacked with all those bad feelings, it can come out in angry, frustrated, and—sometimes—dangerous ways.

Sarah didn't think Zack had it in him to do anything bad to John, or anyone else. But at the same time, she didn't really know Zack all that well. How bad did he want to stay here and not move? If John let it slip that they were investigating Zack, if Zack felt cornered like an animal, who knows what he might do to keep the lie going? Sarah wouldn't let that happen.

Sarah enjoyed working in the cool passages of the Pyramid of Djoser. Besides the temperature and keeping an eye on Zack and her brother, she realized that poking around inside the pyramid was a perfect way to search for the doorway that brought them here. She suspected the portal had something to do with the eye of Ra, as she'd been reminded by Zack's necklace. And John had told her what Zack had told him about the story of Ra and traveling on beams of light across space and time. It seemed like a solid lead, but—the pyramid's internal walls were covered in that symbol. Hundreds of them. So, though they'd been hunting intently, Sarah and John hadn't yet found the way back home.

Despite that disappointment, the idea of giving up never even crossed Sarah's mind. And while she searched, and worked, she had to admit that helping with the decorations and the paintings and the subtle yet intricate details of the lavish artwork came second nature to her. The work felt important and it filled the time while they searched. Even walking into the pyramid felt grand, with two statues of Serket—the woman with a scorpion on her head who protected the dead—guarding each side of the tunnel's mouth. Sarah kept wishing she had her phone to take pictures to show Cynthia and Maxine and everyone else back home. Of course, they'd never believe it.

"You should be an interior decorator," John said on the fourth day they labored together in the tunnels, stone dust covering the hairs on his forearms.

"Isn't that what she is already?" Zack asked, half-joking. He brushed some dust from the wall, revealing a hieroglyph work in progress.

While Sarah and John hadn't found the portal back home, neither had they found any smoking gun proving, or disproving, Zack's innocence in the theft and destruction of the statue of Wadjet. But it hadn't been for lack of trying. Working and living so closely with Zack, neither kid could imagine him capable of such deceit. Zack never let slip any evidence that he'd been involved. And if he'd done it, where had he stashed the head?

Sarah knew, though, that everyone had secrets. While monotonously sanding the edge of a wall, her mind drifted to the secret she hadn't told anyone in the world, not even Cynthia or Maxine. At the camp getaway the second-to-last week of sixth grade, Sarah had kissed Sean Owens. On the lips. It made her giddy and warm and even a little shy to think about it. She didn't regret it, but she also didn't feel the need to tell anyone about it. It was *her* secret. Well, it was *their* secret. That thought made her grin again. Then she found herself blushing thinking about another kiss—with Zack.

Did Zack have secrets of his own? Her secret was a natural and lighthearted one. Was Zack's more sinister? Although even if he was the thief, Sarah knew that he would have done so only because he was scared of moving to a new place where he didn't have any friends, where he would be alone, like John had obviously been feeling about their move to Maryland. So she found it hard to completely fault him for it. But still. If Zack was the thief, he'd caused real damage and—

She stopped her train of thought, realizing she was talking herself into a justification for the crime. But wasn't Zack innocent until proven guilty?

No one in all of Saqqara had come forth with any information, so the case was running cold. Imhotep had mostly moved on, not mentioning it at night at home or during the day at work. His focus remained solely on getting the project done.

Sarah shook her head, throwing rock dust into the air. It tickled her nose and made her sneeze.

"I'm going to get some air," Sarah said, grabbing one of the oil lamps from its fixture in the wall.

"Can I come?" John asked, standing and dusting himself off.

Sarah looked at John, then threw her eyebrows toward Zack working on the far wall. Shouldn't one of them keep an eye on Zack at all times? But at the same time, should she leave John alone with him?

John walked over to Sarah and patted her on the back. "I need some air. Zack's fine." Then, louder, he added, "You want to come, Zack?"

Zack pulled the cloth covering from his mouth and nose. He held up a mallet and chisel. "I'm gonna keep working. I want to finish this one before dinner."

Sarah gave John another *look*.

"You can stay if you want. I'm going out." John trudged up the tunnel toward the outside.

John went about ten steps, while Sarah stayed, watching Zack work.

"Ah, I'm being silly," she said to herself, then turned to go.

"What?" Zack shouted to her.

She stopped and said back to him, "Nothing. Be back in a few minutes."

Zack waved and went back to work.

Sarah jogged up the slope to catch John.

"You still think he's hiding something?" John asked once they were outside in the blazing sun. He used the cloth that had been around his mouth to wipe the instant sweat from his brow.

"I'm sure he is," Sarah said. "But I don't know if that makes him the saboteur."

Sarah walked around the corner of the pyramid from the entrance, using the angle of the sun and the big blocks to get a bit of shade.

John moaned. "We get fresh air up here, but scorching heat. And dust and darkness down there, but it's cool."

"It's pretty neat working on the decorations in the pyramid," Sarah said. "I never knew there was so much craftsmanship on the inside. I mean, the outside is just a big blob in the desert."

"I guess you can't judge a pyramid by its cover," John said, sniggering.

Sarah groaned. "Or maybe it's what's on the inside that counts?"

"Oh!" John made the sound of a drumroll and cymbal crash. "She's here all week, ladies and gentlemen."

Sarah took a bow. "Would still be nice to find that portal."

John swallowed hard. "Are you losing hope we'll find it?"

Sarah chuffed. "Never! We'll find it, Johnny."

"I'm thirsty," John said.

"Me too," Sarah agreed. "We should have brought one of those water jugs with us."

"Yeah, that was kinda silly to leave it down in the tunnel." John scratched his head. "Well, back at it?"

Sarah nodded.

Just as she turned the corner of the pyramid to head back to the tunnel entrance, she stopped suddenly in her tracks and squeezed back behind the wall.

"What is it?" John asked.

"Shh!" Sarah put her finger to her lips. "Look."

They both leaned their heads around the corner.

Someone in a black hooded robe stood at one of the statues of Serket with a chisel and mallet. He whacked into the stone at the base of the neck and her head fell off, landing with a heavy thud in the sand.

Sarah gasped. The hooded person looked to be about Zack's height. Had Zack come to this statue to steal its head as soon as Sarah and John stopped watching him?

The saboteur picked up the head in a black cloth and moved toward the tunnel entrance.

CHAPTER NINE

Traitors Among Us

JOHN

John didn't think twice, though maybe he should have. He burst from their hiding place around the corner of the pyramid and walked with quick, firm steps through the sand toward the saboteur, pointing, yelling, "Hey! Stop!"

The thief didn't hear him and disappeared into the tunnel.

John ran after the thief.

"John!" his sister hissed. "Careful!" He could hear her close behind him.

With no regard for what lay inside, and no oil

lamp to light his way—he realized too late he'd left it sitting on the wall outside when they came up for air—John plunged into the darkness of the pyramid.

He had to slow down after only a few steps lest he smash his face into a wall in the pitch black. Using his hand to guide his way, he moved downward.

"Up ahead," Sarah whispered. "Light."

Sure enough, the glimmer of an oil lamp. As they approached, they could see the robber crouched down and fiddling with the stolen art in the sack of cloth. There was another burlap bag, smaller, on the ground.

When the thief stood up to walk away, John shouted, "Hey!"

The thief, startled, turned abruptly and looked toward John and Sarah, but the face was still shrouded in darkness. The light cast by the oil lamp threw long shadows across the ceiling of the small tunnel.

Now that John had gotten the thief's attention, he wasn't quite sure what to do with it. Thinking quickly on his feet, he said, "The police are on their way. Don't move!"

"Ha, nice try," the thief spoke, a male's voice, but low and gravelly as if he were trying to disguise it. "They call them guards here, not police." The thief stood, the severed head at his feet, the other smaller burlap sack in his hand. He untied the strings holding the small bag closed.

"Sarah, let the *guards* outside know we've caught the thief."

"He's right, you know," Sarah said. "The police are right outside."

"Then why don't you get them?" the thief croaked.

"Maybe I will!" Sarah huffed.

"Maybe this will slow you down." The thief tossed the sack toward them. It landed close to John, with Sarah right behind him.

Springing from the sack, a dozen agitated scorpions skittered across the floor toward John and Sarah.

Sarah shrieked. John's breath stuck in his throat and he couldn't say anything, but he shuffled his feet backward until he ran into Sarah.

"Move!" John yelled as the deadly scorpions

neared, their claws pinching the air, their stingers bobbing on their tails like they were hungry for a fight.

Sarah grabbed John's wrist and they both started running.

John skidded to a halt and wriggled out of Sarah's grasp. She stopped too, looking back at him, then down to the ground at the scorpions. They moved dreadfully fast for such small creatures.

"What're you doing?" she pleaded. "Let's go!"

"Get help," John said. He turned around, his back to Sarah.

"What're you doing?" Sarah repeated, louder, intense fear and confusion in her voice.

Without an answer, John ran *toward* the scorpion horde blocking the hall. As his foot was about to smash into the first of the dangerous bugs, he pushed himself off the ground, his other foot landing squarely against the wall in a move that propelled him farther down the passage. He tucked his head in his arm and collided hard against the ground on the opposite side of the marching scorpions. Onto his feet in a crouch, the scorpions

careening down the hall away from him and toward Sarah, John turned his head to see the thief.

The thief stopped laughing and picked up his
stolen prize, then bolted into a side passage. Before he entered, he stopped with one hand on the
wall, the other holding the statue's head like a
football.

When the thief took another look at John pursu-
ing him, this time he was careless. The lamp lit his
face, shining bright into one eye. John recognized
him. It was the young man on the rolling team, the
man who had first told Imhotep about the robbery.
The man with green eyes.

Aten.

Aten jumped into the side passage.

John closed in on him, but knowing that Aten
had taken a turn down a dead end, he slowed.
Could it be a trap? Would John round the corner
and get clobbered over the head by Aten's hammer?

Suddenly the danger of what he was doing became real.

"Aten!" John yelled. "I know it's you. Sarah
went to get the guards. I don't want—"

From where Aten had disappeared, a blinding flash of white light burst from the side tunnel, brighter than lightning. It hurt John's eyes and he cringed, though the effect ceased as soon as it started.

"Aten?"

That flash. It was just like the one that had brought him and Sarah here. Could it be the same?

John approached the junction for the side passage with slow, methodical steps, trying to listen for any movement at the same time. When he rounded the corner, he wasn't surprised at what he saw, but he felt like he should have been. At the end of the corridor, there was no sign of Aten. His oil lamp rested on the ground, flickering all alone.

"John!" It was Sarah, faintly from the main tunnel. It made John jump.

"I'm okay!" he yelled to his sister. "Sarah, come here. You've got to see this."

Sarah rounded the corner. "What is it?"

She looked beautiful and tender and strong, and John felt an overwhelming sense of pride in his sister, and in himself. The emotions took hold and John went to her and hugged her. She acted surprised, but hugged him back and kissed him on the crown of his head.

"How'd you get past the scorpions?" John asked.

"They followed me right out of the tunnel and into the sunshine," Sarah said. "I considered keeping one as a pet, but I don't think Mom would allow it."

"Speaking of Mom, I think I have a clue how we might see her again." John smiled, eager to get his sister's help in deciphering the riddle.

"Well, don't make me beg!"

"Did you see that flash?"

"Yes," Sarah said. "Just a second ago. It blasted up the tunnel like a ray gun."

"I think it came from there," John said, pointing to the dead-end passage. "I chased Aten in here and then there was the flash and I came in, but he wasn't here and I just saw this lamp and then I heard you and I thought maybe—"

"Slow down," Sarah said, holding her brother by the shoulders. "Start over. Aten?"

John dismissed the question with a quick exhale from his nose. "That doesn't matter. Yes, it was

Aten in the hood. The thief. But what's important is how he escaped."

"So, it wasn't Zack? I mean, we left him in the tunnel and I thought—the hammer and chisel, the hood—" She stood silent for a minute, processing. "You're saying Aten stole the head, then came into this dead end, and then the flash of light made him disappear?" Sarah was putting it together. "So Zack is innocent." A smile graced her lips.

"I think so," John said. "I mean, I know so. That's what happened. That's what I'm trying to tell you. Something with this tunnel, it's connected somehow to the cave in the forest where we came from. It's our way home, Sarah."

"So if the flash of light happened, could we be . . ." Sarah trailed off, her eyes widening.

"Home?" John felt the hairs on his arm rise.

At the same time, their heads turned to look back toward the exit to the outside world.

"What about Zack?" Sarah asked.

"What about him? He's still down there. Sarah, what if we're really home?" John smiled, revealing his one dimple, and took off sprinting toward the exit.

A second later, Sarah closed in on him, running fast.

"I think I smell the forest!" John yelled, his feet slapping up the stone slope.

"I can't wait to tell Mom and Dad about this!" Sarah shouted, her red hair bouncing behind her.

They burst out of the tunnel into the sunlight and landed . . . in sand.

John fell to his knees, out of breath and choking back the emotion of the last few minutes. The thief, the flash of light, thinking they were home only to have that hope dashed—

Sarah slumped into a cross-legged position next to him, sulking. John punched the sand.

Images of home and Mom's fresh-baked chocolate chip cookies and a hug from Dad, his sweaty scent after working in the yard—John missed it all. The sand stretched for miles around and he felt imprisoned by its expansive loneliness. He tottered forward onto all fours and sucked in a lungful of air.

Sarah leaned over and wept silently too, her hair blocking her face. Tears fell into the hot golden sand, rolling down the tiny hills.

"Hey, guys." It was Rich, coming from around the corner of the pyramid with Ella.

"Hey," John replied, sullen. He sat up and tossed some sand.

Sarah sniffled and wiped her nose on her sleeve.

"You all right?" Rich asked, taking a knee near Sarah.

She leaned back and revealed her wet face for all to see. "No."

"Oh no," Ella said, ducking down to comfort Sarah. "What happened?"

"I'll tell you what happened," John said, anger clipping his words. "She went off where she wasn't supposed to and now we're stuck in this place."

Sarah narrowed her eyes and shot her brother an evil stare, but her chin quivered.

John stood, his hands balled up, sand draining out of each clenched fist. "That's right." He pointed at his sister. "If you had listened to me, we wouldn't be in this mess!"

"John, don't—" Sarah whispered.

"You're always doing whatever you want without thinking about me and I'm tired of it. This time you went too far, Sarah. Literally. We're stuck here, away from Mom and Dad and our friends and our school, and we're working on a freakin' pyramid!" John could feel the anger pouring out of his mouth and he didn't like it, but he couldn't stop it. "It's all your fault!" He kick-stamped his foot, sending a burst of sand up and toward Sarah's face.

Ella gasped and turned with Sarah, shielding themselves from the sand flying at them.

Sarah shook herself out of Ella's hug and stood toe-to-toe with John, a full head taller than him. He looked up at her.

"You're just a scared little boy. If you don't live a little, you'll never live at all!" Sarah scoffed.

"Shut up, Sarah!" As soon as he said it, he knew it was bad. Those were banned words in the Tidewell house.

Sarah huffed. "Scaredy cat, scaredy cat, you're just a little scaredy cat." She whined a song and rotated her fists at her eyes in the universal symbol of crying.

The pressure in John's throat and behind his eyes was immense. The anger felt red-hot and the desire to cry from his sister's hurtful words was like a dam wanting to burst. He looked over and saw their friends. Ella had her hand over her mouth. Rich looked away, not meeting his gaze.

Zack emerged from the pyramid and blew out his lamp. He halted, seeing Sarah's sandy cheeks and John's irate scowl.

"Just—just—" John stammered. He couldn't find the words. Communicating while angry and frustrated and in the heat of the moment could be so hard for him. Add to that the embarrassment of a public spat in front of all their new friends. The pressure popped like a burst valve and he screamed in Sarah's face, then took off running into the desert toward the Nile.

John didn't know if Sarah was following, but he hoped she wasn't. He didn't look back. The sound of his own heartbeat and heavy breathing drummed around in his head, drowning out every other sound but those coming from his memories. He thought back to making the fort in the woods with her. Or one time at school, she had simply smiled at him and tousled his hair. But she was in fifth grade at the time, and he was in third grade, and his friends had all thought it was pretty great that he had such a cool older sister. He had been proud to be her brother.

Had been.

John knew deep down in his core that his sister loved him, but that's also why she could make him so sad, so frustrated. There was no feeling in the world quite like the loneliness of being made fun of by Sarah. They were a team. They knew each other's secrets and helped each other out. Sometimes, it felt like them against the world. But since Sarah had gone on to middle school, it seemed like they hung out less and less. She closed her bedroom door more often. She didn't want to play with John as much.

John didn't like to think about the idea that he and Sarah wouldn't be together forever. The thought of being alone felt scary. John really didn't like being scared.

Right now, he felt scared *and* alone.

CHAPTER TEN

Danger Lurks Beneath the Surface

JOHN

After walking for a few minutes, John crested a dune, the bank of the Nile coming into view. Set back from the river, a field showed signs of a recent harvest: low-cut stalks, chaff strewn about, small birds pecking at the leftovers. Maybe the barley Hatmehit had prepared in her tilapia stew?

The sparkling water looked as azure as the bright blue sky on a day clear of clouds. The river beckoned. John raced down the slope of the dune. Not anticipating correctly the steep angle relative to his speed, he stumbled head over heels down the hill. At first, the shock of falling headfirst jolted his senses with fear. But his body met the sand softly, and as he rolled and rolled, the momentum forced a smile to his lips and a laugh from his throat. Next thing he knew, John was whooping from the carefree fun of it.

At the water's edge, John waded up to his knees in the water. The rushing river was a welcome reprieve from the heat of Ra. He chuckled at how he was fitting in, calling the sun Ra instead of just "the sun."

John stepped further out into the water and bent over to splash his face and head. Why hadn't they come down here swimming before?

He took another step, his toes squelching into the muddy silt. He thought about the nutrients in the soil feeding the barley, which went into the stew Hatmehit made that fed him. It reminded John that he'd talked to his mom about starting a garden. Grow some tomatoes and basil and make his own marinara. *Little Chef.* She'd said, "Wait until Maryland, then we can start a plot."

John sighed. Another step into the river. The current tugged on his body and he staggered a bit.

A little two-step dance shuffle and he regained his footing. A pair of beautiful birds floated down out of nowhere and landed in the shallows. They resembled ducks, or geese, somewhere in between those two in size. They wore accent feathers of a lovely golden brown, and their eyes were ringed with a deep velvet red.

A sudden rush of cold water swirled around John, making him shiver despite the heat.

Was that a fish he felt flutter by his toe? John looked down into the murky water. He couldn't see his own knees, the roiling current churning up the sediment. John staggered again from the intense flow and thought he better return to shore. This dip and the time alone had felt cleansing and that was enough. There's no way he had it all figured out between him and his sister, but he'd calmed down enough to go back to the group.

John lifted one knee when a burst of water in the shallows surprised him, knocking him off balance. The sudden uprising tore open the surface of the river and lunged toward the birds at the water's edge. The geese with the red-ringed eyes lurched back and extended their wings. Massive teeth-lined jaws ripped out of the water and snapped down on one bird, crunching its wing and torso in its bite.

The Nile crocodile whipped its head back and forth, in the same thrashing death dance his kind had done for millions of years. After three quick tosses of its head, the bird ceased floundering and the crocodile turned to John.

John had watched the three-second scene while wobbling for his footing in terror, but when the crocodile's eye looked at him—*looked at him!*—John let out a yelp and his brain ordered his body to run. *Run!*

He leaned forward and pushed with his foot, but it slipped and his arms splayed out and he splashed into the river, dunking his head. The water wasn't cold, yet it stole his breath away. He kicked his feet to bounce to the surface.

"*Run!*" his brain was screaming.

John's kicking feet didn't touch sand, disorienting him. Only water swished between his toes. He splashed his hands and saw that the current had sucked him farther away from shore in the blink of an eye.

"Help!" he screamed. "Hel—" A wave pummeled into his head and filled his mouth, drowning out his cry. He was underwater, but he needed to breathe. Fear gripped his body and tensed every muscle. He thrashed around, not sure if he was upside down or right side up. Opening his eyes, he could only see muddy water. He needed to breathe!

Taking a guess, he propelled himself forward.

John bobbed into the air and slapped his arms on the surface of the water. The sun blinded him, but he was glad to see Ra. He sputtered dirty water and took a breath, only to have another wave fill his mouth with more water.

He didn't try to scream again. Was he too frightened even to scream?

He spit, then sucked in an ounce of new air. He held it in. A wave picked him up and for a miraculous second he was floating on his back, staring up at the sun, almost as if it were a casual summer vacation pool day.

A weird calm flushed over him and he stopped worrying about what might happen. It was like playing basketball with the score tied and one minute left on the clock. You don't think about what *might* happen, you just act. You're not consciously aware of the players around you, or the ball in your hands, or the angle of your opponent's foot indicating the direction he might run—you just act. It's like a hyperawareness of the present moment.

John tilted his head up and saw the shore.

Swim. He saw the word flash in his mind.

The crawl stroke. I know the crawl stroke, he thought.

Without commanding his arms to do so, they swung through the air and his legs kicked the water, churning up a froth behind him. It wasn't graceful, but it got him gliding through the water and over the waves, his body angled toward the shore.

The shore. The birds. The croc! Having almost drowned, the other pressing danger of his situation came flooding back and made him shiver with fear. There was a crocodile in the water. Probably more than one. He scanned for the telltale scaly hide, but couldn't see anything besides sprays of rolling water. No sign of the croc.

Though it could be submerged.

Can't do anything about that, he thought, pumping his legs and arms even harder.

"Grab the—" John heard half of a sentence during one of his breaths, his ear going underwater blocking the rest. He looked toward the shore through blurry vision and saw a person holding something out toward him, a long pole.

He reached out and knocked it with his palm but missed.

"Hurry!" the voice yelled, a boy.

"There's a crocodile!" another voice yelled, a girl.

John reached out again through the churn of the river rapids and grabbed hold of the pole. It was a stick. A branch, slick from being worn down by the river's natural rock tumbler.

"It's getting closer!" the girl screamed.

John's grip slipped off the branch and his hand smacked down on the surface of the water. His head went under and he took in a mouthful of gritty river. His foot kicked down and made contact with the bottom. He was close!

Another kick into the dirt and he launched himself even closer to the shore.

Then hands reached under his armpits and pulled him farther up onto the sand, his legs dragging in the water.

"Farther!" the boy yelled.

John coughed and gained his feet and jogged out of the shallows with the girl, her arm around his body helping him on. He glanced back to see the swirl of the crocodile's scaly tail swish away from them deeper into the river.

About ten lumbering steps up the shore, they both collapsed. The sand felt scorching hot on his bare stomach and he loved it. The feeling of solid earth underneath him, the sand in his hands. He coughed up what felt like a bucket of fresh water, then breathed and sat up.

"John!" Sarah wrapped her arms around her brother. She squeezed with such force that John thought his ribs might crack. Without letting up, Sarah said, "John, I'm so sorry. I didn't mean any of that stuff. I was just frustrated and—"

"I'm sorry too." John tried to hug her, but she had his arms pinned so he could only pat her back with tiny T. rex forearms.

"Thought we might have to wrestle a crocodile there for a minute!" Zack said. John could see now that they had all come—Sarah, Zack, Rich, and Ella.

"That was amazing how you swam like that," Rich said. "Can you teach me?"

John laughed. "Sure, but can we do it without the crocodile?"

They laughed.

"Let's go home," Zack said.

"Yeah, that'd be nice," John said. "Wouldn't it, sis?"

Sarah looked John in the eye. "We'll find it. We have to be close." She tousled his drenched hair.

"Let's get you a clean shendyt," Zack said. "If I were you, I'd have soiled myself with that croc hunting me down."

John let out a nervous-but-happy laugh. Zack tossed the stick into the water and watched it float downstream, while Rich and Ella started off toward the village.

"We need to go back to the pyramid," John said to Sarah.

"What? Why?" Rich asked, turning back toward

them.

"Yeah, you nearly died!" Ella said. "I think you can take the rest of the day off."

Sarah nodded at John, then said to the other kids, "It's about the robber."

"What d'you mean?" Zack took his eyes away from the floating stick.

"The saboteur. The thief. We know who took the head of Wadjet," John said. "Because we saw him take the head of Serket too."

"I saw the broken statue when I came out of the pyramid," Zack said. "Near the entryway, right?"

"It was Aten," Sarah said.

"What? How—how do we know it wasn't you?" Zack said, his eye squinting in an accusing stare. Rich and Ella both looked at Zack, then at Sarah, the tension increased.

"Unbelievable!" Sarah said.

"Is it?" Zack asked. Turning to Rich and Ella, he continued, "I was working in the tunnel. They said they needed a break and went outside. Next thing I know there's a bright flash of light and I come up to investigate and they're having a big fight and I see the head of the statue is gone. How do you explain that?"

"Where'd they put the head?" Ella said.

"I saw him," John said. "It's Aten."

"How do we know you're not just covering for your sister?" Zack said.

"I saw you the other night, Zack." Sarah crossed her arms. "When I woke up and heard about the sabotage for the first time, I thought it was you who did it. You have the motive—you don't want to move—and I saw you sneak out of the house in the middle of the night."

Zack's cheeks flushed red. "You—saw that?"

"Yeah, and you had a hood on and you were looking around very suspiciously. You looked guilty, Zack. But I gave you the benefit of the doubt. *We* did. I told John"—she put her arm around her brother's shoulder—"and we decided you were innocent until proven guilty."

"Why'd you sneak out, Zack?" Ella asked, her innocent voice teetering on disappointment.

"Are you and Aten working together?" Rich asked, crossing his arms. He was the biggest kid of the group, and John saw in his stance a tougher side of him.

"What? No, that's not it." Zack tried to chuckle it off. "I just—"

"What, Zack?" John asked. "You just what?" The thought that Zack was working with Aten hadn't occurred to either him or Sarah, but now he had to wonder. But no, John clearly saw Aten working by himself. Although, that didn't mean they hadn't worked together on the first robbery. Maybe Aten was greedy and wanted more and Zack wanted out. Maybe Zack was in trouble, in over his head.

John's thoughts were interrupted by a loud sigh from Zack.

"You guys'll think it's silly," Zack said.

"Try me." Rich flexed his crossed arms.

"I—I like to come down to the river at night and watch Khonsu's reflection," Zack said, looking out on the Nile. "The traveler." Zack gave a half smile, seeming nervous about his story. John had to wonder if he was nervous because he was embarrassed by the story, or because he was lying.

"Who's Khonsu?" Sarah asked.

"The moon disk that travels across the night sky," Ella answered. "He protects travelers."

"And," Zack added, "the best time to travel is

on a crescent moon. I come to this shore to watch the moon disk's reflection travel across the river and think about how my family is soon going to make that same trip across the Nile. We were on schedule to make the move at the time of the crescent moon. But the theft throws us off."

Based on Zack's quick, fluid response, and how easy he held his body, John sensed that Zack was in fact telling the truth. Moving was hard. John knew all about how that feels. He looked at Sarah, who was watching Zack tell his story, her head bobbing slightly in agreement. John could tell that Sarah believed Zack too. If coming down to the Nile at night was how Zack was coping with his big upcoming transition, well, then good for him. John thought maybe he should try something like that when he got back home.

If I ever do get back.

Practically echoing John's thoughts, Zack added, "And I don't know if we'll ever come back after we move away." Zack wiped his nose. He wasn't crying, but John could tell that maybe he wanted to. "To Saqqara, I mean. I'm going to miss you guys."

"Zack," Ella said. "That's sweet."

Rich relaxed his posture and gave Zack's shoulder a playful punch. "Aw, we're going to miss you too. But it'll give us a good excuse to go visit the other side of the Nile."

"I've always wondered what's over there," Ella said, a twinkle in her eye.

"With the theft today—of Serket's head—do you think that will put you back on a schedule to move during the crescent moon?" John asked.

"What're you insinuating?" Zack shot back. "You still think I'm the thief?"

"No!" John honestly hadn't intended any slight, but he could see how his comment could have been taken the wrong way.

"I think he was just trying to be nice," Sarah said, smirking at her brother. Then to Zack she said, "I believe you, Zack. You're not the thief. Do you believe that I didn't do it? I'd have nothing to gain by stealing the statue, and everything to lose."

"Yeah." Zack shook his head. "I don't think it was you. I guess it's just easier to point the finger at the outsiders, the people who are different from us, than it is to think that someone you trust has betrayed you. Someone my father trusts. Aten has worked with him for years. I don't know why he would do such a thing to us."

"We're gonna find out," John said, then started walking up the dune away from the river and back toward the village.

Sarah ran to catch up to him. "Aren't we going to see if we can find a way back to Mom and Dad? We know which tunnel it is now."

"Definitely," John said. "But shouldn't we help our friends first?" He kicked his thumb back at Zack and Rich and Ella. "And Imhotep. And Hat-mehit."

"It's the least we can do," Sarah said. "But you've already told them it was Aten."

"I was the lone witness. It's my word." Saying it out loud filled John with conviction. His heart ached with a desire to go immediately back into that pyramid and try to figure out how to invoke the magic of Ra to transport him and Sarah back to their own time and place. But the words of Hat-mehit echoed in his mind:

Respect is hard won and easily lost.

John knew that if he left Egypt now without giving his testimony to Imhotep about the traitor in their midst, it would haunt him for the rest of his life. If they could get the magic to work and they got home, who knew if it would be able to bring them back to Egypt again? John thought this might be his only chance to do the honorable thing and help stop the saboteur.

CHAPTER ELEVEN

Innocent Until Proven Guilty

JOHN

"Father!" Zack yelled, running down a gravel path toward an open-air structure. Four massive etched columns held up lumber supports that criss-crossed overhead, upon which rested palm fronds that offered shade from Ra. Sarah and Rich followed Zack, with John and Ella farther behind.

Inside his working area, Imhotep stood over a table pointing to a piece of papyrus and discussing something with his team. Nearby, Hatmehit spoke to an old man with gray hair and a gray beard, dressed in a long flowing robe. The old man put his face toward the sky and smiled, breathing in deeply with eyes closed.

"Father!" Zack yelled again.

Hearing his son's cry, Imhotep turned abruptly and met Zack on the path. Hatmehit rushed over as well.

Zack bent over, panting. The rest of the kids skidded to a stop.

Sarah stared at Zack in amazement. "You're a fast"—she took a big breath— "runner!"

"What is it, son?" Imhotep asked, his forehead crinkled with concern. "It looks like you're running for your life in the Heb-Sed. You know we have a special courtyard for that over there." Imhotep grinned, pointing to an oval track.

"Heb-Sed?" John whispered to Ella.

"Every three years our pharaoh has a re-crowning ceremony," she said. "He runs that track in front of the highest members of our society to prove he's fit to rule. If he runs without stopping, he's crowned for another three years."

"And if he fails?" John asked.

Ella gave him a look like the fate was obvious.

"Banished?" John asked.

"Sacrificed," Ella said. "To make way for a more fit successor."

"Yikes," John said.

"Okay, we all know Heb-Sed," Hatmehit said. "But why are you in such a big hurry? What's the matter?"

"We know who the thief is," Zack blurted out.

"That's right," Sarah said. "John saw him."

"He cut off the head of the Serket statue," Ella chimed in.

"We gotta get him!" Rich said, punching his own palm with his fist.

"Wait a minute, children. Hold on." Imhotep waved his hands in a *slow down* gesture, patting the air. "What's this about the thief, Zack?"

Zack pointed to his new friend. "Tell him, John."

"Yes, tell me, John," Imhotep said, crossing his arms. "Who is the thief?"

"Aten, sir." John said it plainly, and it felt good to get it off his chest.

"Aten?" Hatmehit asked. "Did I hear that right?"

John nodded.

"Aten?" Imhotep laughed. "He's one of my

most loyal men. I've known him since he was a child. Why are you accusing him of this?"

John deflated a little, felt his legs shake like they had when he saw the crocodile look at him. Then he remembered how not worrying about the outcome had calmed him, had saved him.

He had nothing to fear from Imhotep. John knew what he saw and he was here to help. If Imhotep didn't believe him, that was Imhotep's problem.

"I saw him at the pyramid," John said, his voice firm. "He cut off the head of one of the statues at the entrance—"

"Of Serket," Ella added.

"Yes, Serket." John smiled at Ella, acknowledging the support.

"You're one hundred percent certain it was Aten?" Imhotep said, his forefinger now tapping the cleft in his strong chin.

"I mean, *Aten*?" Hatmehit said, incredulous, more a question to Imhotep than to John.

"One hundred percent, sir," John said. He pictured the young man in his mind's eye, in the tunnel, with the lamp illuminating his face. It suddenly did seem possible that the shadows could have been playing tricks on his eyes. Was he really one hundred percent certain? Enough to condemn a man?

"Where did he go with the stolen head?" Imhotep asked.

"He, uh—" John looked to his sister.

"Disappeared," Sarah said. Well, it was the truth.

"Yeah, I went after him into the pyramid, but I lost him in the dark," John said.

"You pursued a dangerous criminal—who you say might have been Aten—into the pyramid?" Imhotep asked, one eyebrow raised.

John nodded.

"That wasn't very wise," Hatmehit said. "You should have come to us right away."

"Sorry," John said, but he didn't look down.

"I'm glad you're okay. You're very brave, John-from-across-the-sea." Imhotep put one hand on John's shoulder and gave it a firm squeeze. John swelled with pride. He couldn't remember ever being called brave before. It sounded princely coming from Imhotep's mouth.

"There's a fine line between stupid and brave," Sarah added. "You should have seen the scorpions he jumped over."

"Scorpions?" Imhotep looked to Sarah.

"Yeah," Sarah answered. "He threw a bag of scorpions at us. That's how he got away. I ran out to find help and our Brave John here leapt over the scorpions and somersaulted ninja-style down the tunnel and after Aten."

"Ninja-style?" Zack asked.

John smirked. "Not sure you have those around here."

"They're very agile trained warriors," Sarah said. "Just like John." She winked.

"Ninja John," Ella said, grinning. She seemed to admire John's heroism.

"Scorpions in a bag," Imhotep said. "Very interesting."

"Why?" Zack asked his father.

"My assistant told me that we're missing a dozen scorpions from the group that will be the final placement in King Djoser's chamber," Imhotep said. Then he leaned to John and Sarah and explained that the scorpions represent Serket, who protects the dead, among other things.

"We know," Sarah said.

"Oh." Imhotep looked surprised. "Aten was the last to be seen with the scorpions. I didn't think anything of it, since it's common for him to check on one of the most important aspects of our project. I mean, he helps me with practically all of the operation, so . . ." He trailed off in thought.

Zack seemed to know what his father was thinking. "He betrayed us, Dad."

Imhotep glared at his son. "How could you say that?"

"I don't know why he did it," Zack said. "But he can't be trusted."

"Tell them," Hatmehit said to her husband.

Imhotep scowled. "If what you say is true, it doesn't make sense. Aten has been missing since yesterday morning. No one has seen him."

"Missing?" Rich asked. "That sure is suspicious."

"But wouldn't someone have seen him besides you?" Hatmehit asked.

"Not if he didn't want to be found," Sarah said. "He was wearing a dark hood and ran away from us in a hurry."

"I want to speak to Aten," Imhotep said, clenching his jaw and his fist simultaneously. "We have to find him."

"Can I come with you?" Rich asked, itching for a fight.

"You said you saw him last in the pyramid?" Imhotep said, stepping back toward his team. "I'll assemble the guards and we'll go straightaway."

"Remember, innocent until proven guilty," Hatmehit said.

"That may be a concept too early for this time," Sarah said to John, watching Imhotep rally a group of guards armed with spears and curved swords.

John took Sarah aside and whispered, "We have to go. Now."

"What? Go where?"

"Home," John said. "Back to the dead end in the pyramid, before it's crawling with guards and we don't have another chance."

"Shoot," Sarah said, looking back to the guards talking with each other. Imhotep barked an order and one ran off, presumably to gather more soldiers.

"Dangit, Sarah, we gotta go," John said, pulling his sister on the elbow. Their friends were distracted by the hubbub of the guards.

Sarah stepped toward John, but her body turned to face their friends. "Shouldn't we say goodbye?"

"There's no time," John said. "I'll miss them too."

Sarah gave a little wave that John hoped no one would see.

John added, "There's too much to explain, anyway. They'd never understand."

Sarah frowned and went with John. He didn't like it either, but he knew he was right.

As soon as they left the gravel path, they veered right behind a pillar carved to look like the reeds found down by the river. They had a clear line of sight to the pyramid entrance and could probably make it undetected.

Probably.

CHAPTER TWELVE

A Disappearing Act

SARAH

Sarah watched John push off from their hiding place behind the pillar and she hesitated a moment. Usually, she was the first one to throw caution to the wind, but here John was being the leader. She grinned and took off running after him. John might have a head start, but she'd catch him. Her sense of competitiveness hadn't been left behind in Colorado.

Halfway across the stretch of sand to the pyramid, she hazarded a glance back toward the structure from which they'd come. No one was following. That was good. But given the urgency in Imhotep's commands, she expected troops to surround the pyramid any second now.

Sarah could have passed John when she caught up to him, but instead she kept pace and ran alongside. Well, maybe she pushed ahead just enough to chide John into running a little faster too.

A few seconds later and they both careened into the shadow of the tunnel's entrance. John flopped to the ground, out of breath. Sarah leaned her hands on her knees.

"We seem to be running everywhere lately," Sarah said.

"We can't run down this tunnel in the dark, though." John sat in pitch black, but some of the light from outside lit half his face.

"And we don't have lamps," Sarah realized.

"Yeah," John said, looking up at his sister. "I thought about that too late too. I guess we'll have to feel our way down the passage." She could see in his one lit eye that he expected her to react in fear at that plan. Maybe he wanted some justification for his own fear.

"We'll have to be careful," she said, meeting his desire for an excuse halfway. "But we can do it."

"I know we *can* do it," John said. "I just hope those scorpions are gone."

Or cobras. Or spiders. Or—

Sarah shook her head with a shiver. "We have to try."

John swallowed, the sound of his gulp loud in the quiet, dark tunnel. Then he stood.

Side by side, each of them with one hand on the wall—Sarah on the left with her left hand on the wall and her right hand holding John's hand, and John on the right with his right hand on the wall—they traversed slowly step by aching step into the dark of the tunnel.

"I can't see my nose," Sarah said.

"I can't wait to have some ice cream," John said.

Sarah suddenly pictured home, Mom and Dad pulling out the tubs of ice cream choices, the various shakers of sprinkles, the whipped cream can that you could shoot into your mouth, the chocolate sauce—

"Chocolate sauce . . ." she murmured.

Did John just pick up his pace? Sarah chuckled

at the thought. Driven home by ice cream.

More steps down the tunnel, but it didn't feel like they were moving at all—the darkness didn't change. Sarah looked behind her to the entrance and it did seem farther away. Then the silhouette of a person stepped into the light of the doorway. Lit from behind, the face was hard to make out. She stopped.

"Quiet," Sarah whispered.

"Wha—" John started, but then he silenced himself.

Sarah bent closer to John. She couldn't see him and didn't want to smash into his head, so she stopped probably far short of his ear. Not wanting her voice to carry, she whispered as barely as she could. Air hardly left her mouth.

"Look back," was all she said.

After he looked, John inhaled a quick breath through his teeth. "Shoot."

"Think it's Zack or—" She squinted, but it didn't help much. "Looks like someone bigger than Zack. Maybe Rich?"

"Or a guard?" John said. "But wouldn't they call out?"

"Oh no," Sarah said, hand over her mouth.

"Sarah?"

"What if it's Aten?"

John didn't respond, but she could hear his breath quivering.

A tiny spark and then a glow from an oil lamp looked like a fluttering heart in the silhouette. Sarah was too far away to tell who it was, but it spooked her.

"We should go," Sarah said. John started moving again as soon as she said it.

A few steps later and Sarah looked back again. The silhouette was gone from the doorway, replaced by a bobbing flame careening down the tunnel toward them. It was making much faster time than they were without light. Not too much longer and they'd have an entirely different kind of decision to make. Should she risk calling out to see who was coming down the tunnel toward them?

"We're here," John whispered, then he tugged Sarah's arm into the side passage. "This is where Aten disappeared. At the dead end."

From her memory, she knew this passage was

only about ten steps deep, so she took the first few strides more confidently. Then she slowed with both hands outstretched so she wouldn't bang into the wall.

"Do you remember where the eye of Ra is?" John asked. Sarah could hear the beginnings of panic in his voice.

"It was at about my eye level," Sarah said, feeling around on the wall. Realizing what she said, she chuckled. "Ha. The eye is at eye level. Of course it is."

Her fingers traced the contours of the hieroglyphs and she imagined being blind, working her way through life by touch and memory. And sound: the person coming down the tunnel scuffed a foot and grunted. Another person made a shushing sound.

"Hurry, Sarah!" John whispered. "They're after us!"

"Found it," Sarah said, feeling the familiar almond shape of the eye. "Here we go."

She traced the shape, down to the curlicue, and closed her eyes. She couldn't see anything anyway, but she expected a bright flash to carry them home.

Nothing happened.

"It didn't work," she muttered. "Are you sure this is the one?"

"Yes! Try again!"

"Hello?" A voice very close by.

"Is someone there?" A different voice, trembling.

Shoot! thought Sarah. They'd been too loud. They were inside the pyramid without a light and had crept away from the group without saying anything—it might appear to others that they were trying to hide. Would Imhotep think, as Zack had accused, that they were actually the thieves, trying to throw suspicion off themselves by blaming Aten and then escaping?

Sarah realized she was massaging her neck with one hand, imagining what it might feel like to be decapitated. In her mind, she pictured the eye of Ra, the brow, the iris, the curlicue finish, the line underneath pointing straight down like a knife's edge—

"That's it!" Sarah said. "The line pointing down. I forgot to trace that too."

"Well, do it!" John said.

"I am," Sarah replied. "I'm tracing the whole thing now."

"Sarah, John, is that you?" someone said.

Sarah recognized the voice.

She turned as her finger completed tracing down the last line. "Zack?"

The bright zap of light captured the scene like a photographer's flashbulb. Beyond her brother, standing in the passage at the junction with the dead end, Sarah could clearly see Zack, Rich, and Ella. Zack held a tiny oil lamp, the flame rendered useless in that nanosecond of eye-watering illumination.

Then all went black again. The residual scene faded from Sarah's retinas and all were again in darkness. Deep, dark, blacker than before. The tiny oil lamp wavered as if the light had caused a wind to blow, but Sarah knew it was from Zack's shaking hand.

"What—" Zack started.

"Was—" Rich added.

"That?" Ella concluded.

"What are you doing here?" Sarah asked their friends.

"Why didn't you say something?" John pleaded. "We thought you were Aten coming to murder us."

"We could ask you the same thing," Rich said. "I saw you sneak out and run into the pyramid."

"We followed you in here," Zack said. "But—"

"What was that light?" Ella asked.

"Yeah," Rich said. "What was that magic? It was brighter than Ra!"

"It may have been Ra's magic," John said, stepping closer to Zack. Sarah followed. At least now, up close, they could dimly make out the faces of their friends.

"We may be somewhere far from your home now," Sarah said. She placed a hand on Ella's shoulder. "But you're safe."

"Are you working with Aten?" Rich asked.

"No," John said. His face was set so firmly that Sarah could only look at her brother and nod in agreement. There was nothing more to add.

"Then explain," Rich said.

"I think the best way," Sarah said, "is to show you."

"I hope it worked," John said. "Not like last time."

"This wasn't like last time, John." Sarah put her other hand on John's shoulder. "I could feel it this time, just like when I brought us here. I know it."

Zack shook his head. "What're you talking about?"

"Let's go," Sarah said, and took a few steps up the tunnel. John jogged past her. Zack, Rich, and Ella watched them go.

Sarah turned around and cajoled them. "I promise you it'll be like nothing you've ever seen before."

She watched each of them look to the other, perplexed. Finally, Zack shrugged, and they all followed Sarah toward the tunnel exit.

Sarah didn't run, didn't jog, didn't skip. Her heart beat fast and she felt lightheaded. Something inside of her knew this time was different from the last time they saw the flash, when Aten disappeared, when they'd been so excited and then so disappointed. She knew this time it had to have worked—she felt the sizzle of excitement down to her bones—but something made her temper her enthusiasm. Sarah wanted nothing in the world more than to hug her parents again, but her mind felt fragile at the thought that this could be only a trick like last time. A tease. Her heart felt too sensitive to endure that kind of punch again. If she came out into the light above—which was getting nearer and nearer with every step—and she wasn't back in the Colorado forest, Sarah thought she might just lie down and never get up again. It wasn't that ancient Egypt was so bad, it was just that it wasn't her home. No, it wasn't the *place* she missed. She wanted her family back together again. This journey across space and time had been a wonderful adventure, but if she couldn't share it with her whole family, then something big was missing from her life.

Lifting her head from her thoughts, she saw John stopped in the exit. She couldn't tell if he was in awe and relief at seeing the forest, or in pain and disappointment at the sight of the desert. Behind him wasn't bright sunlight. It was a duller hue, like dusk.

"John?" Sarah asked.

John turned around, tears running down his cheeks. Sarah's heart did one last beat and froze. Her throat constricted. *No, no.*

"You did it, Sarah!" John took her hand and pulled her the last few steps, yanking her from the stupor.

She staggered to the edge of the tunnel—no, it was the mouth of a cave!—and looked out to the evening light through towering pine trees on a steep slope.

It was the most beautiful view of the mountains she'd ever witnessed. The cold air prickled her skin. She sucked it in through her mouth and nose and gulped the scene through wide eyes. The fresh scent of evergreen trees, the rich aroma of the dirt.

Instead of her usual jumping excitement, Sarah fell to her knees.

John laughed and jumped and wailed with joy.

"We're—home," Sarah muttered to herself. "We're home. We did it." She thought she'd never see it again.

"Is this real?" Ella asked.

The question sounded absurd to Sarah. This felt

more real to her than any of the last weeks in the Nile Delta, more real than the smooth stone she rolled to the pyramid, more real than Imhotep and Hatmehit and tilapia barley stew and Aten and all of it—

Sarah turned to Ella, realizing that Ella was now experiencing the amazing feelings of bewilderment that had struck Sarah when she first went through the portal to another time and place completely foreign to her.

"It's okay," Sarah said. "Yes, this is real."

Rich took a step back into the tunnel. "What'd you do to us? This is some sort of black magic!" He ran back into the tunnel.

Zack laughed. "So, this is what you've been hiding. This is your secret."

"We all have them," Sarah said. "I didn't think you'd understand."

"You're definitely right there," Ella said. "I still don't know what's happening."

"This is fantastic," Zack said. "The symbol you traced—"

"The eye of Ra," Sarah said.

"That particular inscription tells the story of Ra

traveling across space and time. His chariot, pulled by beams of light, carries the ka of King Djoser to wherever he wants to go and lets him understand all languages past, present, and future."

"Handy," Sarah said.

"Across space and time," John repeated, remembering the first time Zack had told him the story inside the pyramid. He laughed and ran his hands through his hair. "We did it!"

"I'm guessing Ra has transported us?" Zack asked, a smile on his lips. "Like he does the ka?"

"Does that mean we're—dead?" Ella asked.

John tugged on Sarah's arm. "Come on! We have to go find Mom and Dad."

"John—" Sarah gestured to their friends. "Where's Rich?"

"He'll be back," Ella said.

At that moment, creeping from the shadow of the tunnel, Rich poked his head out. "Ella? I'm scared."

"I absolutely understand," Sarah said. "But you're safe, Rich. I promise."

"I want to go find Mom and Dad," John said

again, impatiently tugging on Sarah's elbow as if he had to go to the bathroom.

"Me too," Sarah said. Then to their friends, she said, "You guys follow us and I'll explain as we go."

"I want to go home," Rich said.

"Me too," Ella said.

"Come on, let's explore a little." Zack stepped away from the tunnel and over to a tree. "I've never seen anything like this. It's so—so—"

"Big!" Ella said, suddenly standing next to Zack and looking up with her head cranked all the way back.

"How do we get home?" Rich asked. "Are we stuck here?"

"We were stuck in ancient Egypt," John said. "Until we figured out the secret to that hieroglyph. The eye of Ra."

"Take me back." Rich shivered. "Now."

"I—" Sarah hesitated. She wanted to go see her parents. But she understood the anxiety Rich was having. If someone had told her the way back when she first landed in Egypt, would she have wanted to go back immediately? Well, probably not, but . . . She smiled at herself.

"I'll teach you how to do it and you can go." Sarah set a hand on Rich's back. He flinched at first, but it seemed to calm him down. He nodded, accepting her offer.

"Rich," Zack said, "don't you want to explore a little first? We've been given a rare opportunity here. Let's see this world! Where—or when—are we, anyway?"

"Colorado. The year is 2019." John paused, scratching the back of his head. "Hm, that's 2019 CE, meaning the 'Common Era.' According to our history books, you're from about 2600 *before* the Common Era, or BCE, so that's almost five thousand years ago."

Ella giggled. Zack's jaw dropped. Rich shook his head in disbelief.

"We're in the future?" Ella said.

"Well, it's the present to us," Sarah said, "but, yeah, the future to you. When we were in Egypt, it was ancient history to us. It was fascinating learning about your culture firsthand. Maybe—"

"Maybe you'd like to learn a little about us now?" John asked. "Since we weren't totally honest with you before."

"I can understand why," Zack said. "This is hard to believe."

"Trust me, I know how you feel," John said, laughing. He patted his hand against Zack's chest.

"Look," Zack said, his eyes on John's watch. "It's moving."

"Hey, look at that, my watch is working again." John laughed a short "*Ha!*"

"There's no sand here," Ella said, scanning the forest.

Sarah laughed, in fact thankful there wasn't sand under her feet for once. "We do have some of that in Colorado, but we're in the high country here. Mountains."

"I've heard of mountains," Rich said, his voice timid. "But only in fables. They're supposed to be full of monsters guarding riches."

"I'd definitely agree with the riches," John said. "And as for monsters, we do have bears and mountain lions and such, but those are animals. To you, they may seem like fantastical beasts, and they're creatures certainly best avoided, but they're not monsters."

John smiled, then gestured to the trailhead. "Can we go now?"

Sarah looked to their friends. Zack and Ella looked to Rich. Rich opened and closed his mouth but didn't say anything.

"Come on, Rich. Just a little while. It'll be fun, and we'll be home in no time." Ella tugged on his tunic. "Please?"

Rich blinked, and his head wavered. Sarah could tell that Ella's big eyes were working on him.

"Just a little while," Rich said.

"Yay!" Ella jumped up. When she came back down, she hit a rock sideways and yelped in pain, twisting her ankle and sliding down the slope.

"Whoa!" John ran over to her and knelt down. "You okay?"

She rubbed at her ankle but wasn't crying.

"Let's get you some ice for that," Sarah said.

"Ice?" Rich asked, kneeling next to Ella as well.

"Frozen water," John said. "It'll take the swelling down. And some ibuprofen for the pain."

"I-bew-pro-fin?" Ella asked.

"Medicine," John said.

Rich put his arm around Ella's back and lifted her with ease. "Let's get this over with."

CHAPTER THIRTEEN

Home for Some

JOHN

"My watch . . ." John didn't finish his thought.

"Yeah, you told us already," Sarah said. "It's working again. Cool."

"But it only shows a little after seven p.m. on the same day we left," John added, his face staring at his wrist in confusion.

"Makes sense if it was frozen all that time, right?"

"I guess," John said. "But look at the sun. It hasn't set yet, like when we left and traveled through that portal."

"Your watch was frozen and it's just a coincidence we're back at the same time of evening, but it has to be a different day," Sarah said, turning right onto the main trail to go down, back to their house.

"Yeah, it's just—" John looked up the trail to the left and paused.

Sarah kept walking down and around a switchback, followed by Rich carrying Ella, then Zack. The Egyptian children walked unsteady on the rocky terrain, and John worried that if Rich took a tumble, he'd toss Ella down the hill, maybe smack into a tree trunk.

"I think Mom and Dad are still hiking up there," John said, more to himself than anyone else. "Like we never left."

"Come on, John. Let's go home," Sarah said without looking back.

John ignored her and yelled up the mountainside. "Mom! Dad!" He cupped his hands around his mouth and yelled again. "Dad! Mom! You there?"

John cocked his ear to listen. Two seconds ticked by.

"John?" It was faint but clear as a bell. The voice of his mother was as sweet as ever.

"You okay?" His father's voice too. "Sarah all right?"

John wanted to yell back, but the lump caught in his throat prevented it. He looked down to Sarah, who had skidded to a stop in her tracks.

"Mom! Dad!" she hollered. "We're here! We're home!"

Sarah leapt up the hillside, ignoring the trail and scrambling straight over the fallen trunks and knee-high boulders. The giddiness surged into John as well, and he bounded up the slope too, leaving their friends behind.

"Wait!" Zack yelled.

But John and Sarah kept running, as fast as their legs could pump on the steep incline.

"Honey, are you all right?" Mom jogged down the trail, a worried look pulling her cheeks back. Dad, right behind her, stomped down the trail heavy-footed, letting gravity propel him.

Mom stopped short of Sarah. "Honey, what are you wear—"

Even though Sarah's momentum was slowed by

the upward angle of the trail and her own heavy breathing, she bowled right into her mom's open arms so hard that her mom had to throw a foot back to keep from falling over.

John wrapped his arms around them both, and when Dad hugged the group, John squeezed into his dad's body so tightly that all he could smell was his dad's sweaty musk. He inhaled deeply and thought he was never so glad to smell such stink.

"Where are your clothes?" Dad asked, pulling away and looking John in the eye. "What happened?"

John's smile felt so wide it might crack his cheeks. He wiped a tear from one eye and thought about where to begin. "We went in the cave and there was a bright flash and then we came out in ancient Egypt and I nearly got bit by a cobra and then there were these giant spiders on Zack's back, and Sarah was on the rolling team, and I jumped over scorpions, and Sarah saved me from a crocodile and—"

"You saved yourself from that croc," Sarah interrupted. "I pulled you out of the river, but you're the one who swam all the way to shore despite that wicked current. You were super brave, little bro."

John beamed at his sister. "I couldn't have survived that trip without you, sis." His heart was so full of overflowing joy that he didn't know how else to express the gratitude that tingled his skin. Without his sister, that adventure would have been very different.

"What are you talking about?" Mom asked. "Crocodile?"

"In the Nile," John said, realizing that though he said it with a straight face, it must have sounded extremely bizarre to his parents. Crazy or not, it felt good to tell them. To be here, with them. He wanted to tell them everything.

"Something happened in that cave," Sarah said, shaking her head. "I don't know how to explain it. But we traveled—"

"Through time," John said.

"To ancient Egypt," Sarah said. "The time of the very first pyramid. King Djoser. Saqqara. Imhotep."

Their dad smirked and rubbed his beard.

"Amazing."

"You don't believe us," John said. "But it's true."

"Uh-huh," Mom said, exchanging a glance with Dad. "I'm sure they didn't stash those clothes up here to play a trick on us. A trip to ancient Egypt, right? That must have been so—"

"Hot," Sarah said. "And sandy." The whole family burst out laughing.

John was old enough to recognize when his parents didn't really believe him and were only playing along, but he didn't care right now. He knew it sounded too fantastical to believe, so he didn't blame them. The important thing is they were home. They were safe and home.

"Hello?" Ella said in her meek voice.

Well, some of them were home, anyway.

"Dad, Mom, meet Ella," Sarah said. "And that's Rich and Zack."

Dad looked the new kids up and down, obviously distracted by the cloth wrapped around the boys' hips like ancient shorts, their bare chests, Ella's tube dress, Zack's necklace of the eye of Ra in jade. Their brown and deeply tanned skin probably made them look like they were from California or Florida.

"Well, looks like everyone is in on the joke. Nice to meet you," Dad said. "I'm Isaac Tidewell." He stuck out a hand.

"Hello," Mom said. "I'm Maryanne." She stuck out a hand also.

The kids looked at the outstretched hands in amusement.

"Ah, I remember—the shake," Zack said to Sarah.

Sarah nodded with a smile.

Zack grasped Mom's hand and gave it a firm tug.

"Ouch, that's quite a handshake you have there," Mom said. "Nice to meet you . . ." She trailed off, waiting to hear his name.

"This is Zack," Sarah said for him.

"Zachariah," he corrected her.

"It's a pleasure meeting you," Mom said, tilting her head in a slight bow.

"I'm glad," Zack said. Then he released her hand as quickly as he'd grabbed it and took Dad's hand firmly.

"Well, that *is* quite a handshake," Dad said.

They made the rounds after that, Rich introducing himself by his full name of Netjerichet ("Rich," Sarah interjected) and Ella announcing herself as Ellasandra ("We call her Ella," John said). Rich didn't shake hands, since he still had Ella in his arms.

"Never heard that one before," Dad said about Rich's full name. "What ancestry is that?"

"My family is from Egypt, like all families," Rich said, as if it were a silly question.

"Oh, right," Dad said, grinning and stroking his beard. "I forgot. Ancient Egypt. Gotta keep that going." He rolled his finger in a circle.

"Ellasandra—I like that, such a beautiful name. Why is Rich carrying you?" Mom asked.

"You can put me down," Ella said to Rich. Then to Mom, she said, "I hurt my ankle when we came out of the pyramid. Hurts to walk, but I can stand okay."

"I'm sorry to hear that," Mom said. "Pyramid?"

"Uh, the cave," John said.

"Where are your parents?" Mom asked Ella.

"Do you live around here?" Dad asked, twirling his finger down toward the houses.

Zack chuckled. "We're from Egypt. Well, John told us you call it ancient Egypt."

Dad watched Zack for a second to gauge his reaction, then he laughed and wagged his finger at Zack. He pointed to Sarah and John. "I'm glad you kids are having so much fun making up stories together. I love it. The costumes are a nice touch." He circled his finger around his own clothes. "I used to do some role-playing games when I was younger too."

Mom chuckled, then asked again about their parents. "If Ella is hurt, we should make sure her parents know she's all right. Do you have a phone to call them?" She took out her own phone. "Or do you know their number so I can?"

Ella looked confused. To her, the phone must have looked like only a thin metal box.

"Their parents aren't here," Sarah interjected.

"You can say that again," John muttered under his breath.

"Hiking alone?" Mom asked.

"No," Rich said. "We came with Sarah and John."

Ella leaned on Rich. "Our parents are home.

They said we could explore with John and Sarah," she lied.

"And spend the night," John said, thinking quickly. "If it's okay with you guys, of course."

Dad grunted. "I don't know. We're getting ready to move and the house is kind of a mess right now. You know that, John."

"Please, Dad?" Sarah turned up her charm, which often worked on their dad. "Ella can sleep in my room, and Rich and Zack can sleep in John's room. We have plenty of sleeping bags. Please?" She grabbed her dad's arm and put her head against his shoulder, looking up at him with doe eyes.

"I'm okay with a sleepover," Mom answered. "But I'd like to talk with their parents first."

Sarah twisted her mouth and squinted her eyes. John knew that look. She was scheming something.

"They're—on a date night," Sarah said. "And they said they turn their phones off. So they're probably unreachable."

Mom tilted her head at Sarah. "Still, I'd like to try. I can leave a message with my contact info."

John chimed in, looking at the Egyptian kids. "You guys said you don't have their numbers memorized, right?" He saw his dad's eyes narrow.

"I have it in my phone," Sarah said, smiling a bit too large.

"But let me guess—you don't have it with you?" Dad asked.

"Of course not. Not while we're on a family hike, Dad. Come on, you know better than that," Sarah chided.

"Well," Mom said, eyeing the children. "Odd situation we have here. I guess we should get down off this mountain with our wounded guest. At least we can get her some ice and a wrap. Then Sarah can get us that number, and we can call her parents and make sure they're okay with a sleep-over."

"Exactly!" Sarah said.

That bought them some time, but what were they going to do once they got back to the house?

Once they all started off down the trail, John managed to get Sarah to the side and whispered, "What're we going to do?"

"Don't worry," Sarah said, cool as a cucumber.

"I'm going to call in a favor from Maxine."

"What d'you mean?"

"Maxine has called in sick to school a few times," Sarah said, nodding as if that explained everything.

"I don't get it," John said.

"Maxine has a very adult-sounding voice. I mean, she can fake it well. I'll ask her to do me a favor and pretend to be their mom."

"But doesn't Mom have Maxine's parents' number? Won't she recognize it when you give it to her?" John thought he'd found a hole in Sarah's plan.

"They do have her parents' number. But not Maxine's." Sarah nodded in smug satisfaction. "I need you to distract Mom and Dad for a while when we get home. Give me a chance to call Maxine and prep her. You in?"

"I don't have any better idea," John said. "So yeah, I'm in."

"Operation Sleepover will be a success," Sarah said, grinning.

John smiled back. They made a good team.

"Hey, whatcha talkin' 'bout?" Dad snuck in

between them and looped an arm over each of their shoulders.

"Uh, just bummed we didn't get to see that sunset from Crescent Vista. I know you were excited to see it," Sarah said.

The mention of "crescent" reminded John how Zack had talked about the crescent moon being a good sign for travelers.

"That's all right. There'll be more sunsets," Dad said, smiling at Sarah.

"I want to get home and have some ice cream," John said, licking his lips. "Chocolate sauce . . ." He pretended to drool.

"Think your new friends will want some too?" Dad asked. He moved his hand up to tousle John's hair, then pulled his arm back at the last minute before John even had time to cringe away. "Ah, sorry, Johnny. I know you don't like that anymore. I keep having to remind myself. Be patient with me. Hard to teach an old dog new tricks."

"You're not that old," John said. "You can still learn some new tricks."

His dad laughed at that. "I swear you two look older than when I saw you a minute ago. When you have your own kids, you'll know what I mean. Sometimes I look at you and just . . . Wow." Something took his breath away and he exhaled a heavy sigh. Then said, "I love you two."

"Love you too, Dad." John reached and mussed his dad's hair, laughing while he did it. His dad laughed with him, and John felt a warmth blooming in his chest, spreading into his gut and his cheeks. This was what home felt like.

"Proud of you two," Dad said.

"We know, Dad," Sarah replied.

"Good," Dad said. "But do you know why this time?"

"Um, because we love ice cream?" John joked.

Dad sniggered. "No, because you both make friends so easily. How come we've never met these kids before?"

John skipped a step.

"Don't worry," Dad said. "I don't know what you're cooking, but I can tell that you guys are pretty good friends with those kids. It's like you've known them a long time, and yet I've never met them, which makes me think you just met them on the trail tonight. And already you seem so tight, helping each other out, playing along with each other's stories. It's wonderful." He looked at John. "See? You were worried about losing your best pal, Roman. I get it. Our move might mean you two grow apart—it happens. But what I'm trying to say here is that just look at you. Made new friends one night randomly while on a hike. I can't wait to see who you'll meet in Maryland. I'm proud of you. That's all."

John understood what his dad was fumbling around, and he realized it was true. When they'd started out on this hike, weeks ago, all John could think about was how he didn't want to move, didn't want to be away from his best friend, Roman. And while he did still miss Roman, he missed him less. The times they had were one-of-a-kind, but the times he'd had with Zack and Rich and Ella were one-of-a-kind too. He knew that his friendship with these kids would come to a close, and probably soon. But he'd make new friends. In Maryland or wherever the current of life may take him. As long as he remembered to swim.

"Shared experience and time, Dad," John said.

Dad paused and looked at him. "That is very

wise, son."

They kept walking, quiet for a few moments. A bird trilled its sunset song.

Dad threw his arm around John's shoulder and mumbled, more to himself, "Shared experience and time. I like that."

Dad squinted at John as if seeing him in a new way, or for the first time.

CHAPTER FOURTEEN

The Future Is Now

JOHN

"Ouch!" Ella screamed, lying on the couch in the Tidewells' living room with her leg propped up on a pillow.

Mom retracted the bag of ice with a look of surprise.

"How does that burn without a flame?" Ella asked.

"What're you doing to her?" Rich asked, posturing defensively between Mom and Ella. Zack watched with more interest than fear.

Sarah chuckled and took the ice pack from

Mom. She wobbled it back and forth between her palms. "It's ice, not fire. It's cold, but it feels hot at first. It's okay. It won't hurt you."

"Okay," Ella said, nodding assent to Sarah.

"Guess the water never freezes where you're from?" John asked.

Rich shook his head like he didn't understand.

Gently Sarah placed the ice pack on Ella's ankle. "It'll bite a little, but it won't hurt you. And it'll take the swelling down. Trust me."

Mom raised an eyebrow and grinned. "Staying in character, I see. You're quite good. Are you a part of the theater group in your school?"

"Zack got to go to school," Ella said. She crossed her arms with a frown.

John looked to Zack to explain why Ella was upset.

"She wants to go too," Zack said. "To school."

"Why doesn't she?" Mom asked.

"Because," Zack said, "only boys go to school."

"Only wealthy boys," Rich added, a hint of jealousy in his tone. "I went straight to work on the pyramid when I was eight."

"True. I learned how to read and write in

school." Zack didn't sound ashamed at all of his privilege. "I'm training to be a scribe. That's how I got the honor of helping with the transcription of the stories onto our pyramid's walls. My father took a risk by letting a boy my age have that responsibility. I take it very seriously."

"And you do a great job, Zack," Ella said. "I just wish I could write too. I mean, I love hearing the stories. I just wish I could read them too."

"I can teach you to read!" Sarah said, a big grin on her face. "I love teaching the younger kids at school. We have a program in our middle school where once a week we older kids team up with them to help with a subject. I usually volunteer for the reading duty. Watching someone learn to read, putting the pieces together from scribbles on paper into meaning and stories, and watching their eyes light up when they get it? That's super cool."

"That'd be terrific," Ella said. "Girls are allowed to go to school here? What a wonderful place. Hear that, Zack?" She adjusted the ice pack on her ankle.

Mom laughed. "Oh boy, you kids are having too much fun. I'm going to see if Dad needs any help getting the ice cream ready. Anyone up for Monopoly? We have the National Parks Edition—"

"Maybe tomorrow night, 'kay, Mom?" John said.

"Okay . . ." She gave him a look like she'd never heard him turn down the offer of Monopoly, probably because he hadn't ever done so.

As soon as their mom left the living room, Sarah gave a nod to John and disappeared down the hallway. John heard her bedroom door close and a minute later could hear the low mutterings of Sarah on a phone call. Prepping Maxine to pretend to be the parent of their visitors. It seemed like an impossible plan, but Sarah was good at that kind of thing!

Ella lay back on the couch with her leg propped on a pillow while Zack rolled around on the floor like a dog. John watched Zack enjoying the carpet.

"This rug is amazing," Zack said. "How many sheep do you have?"

"Sheep?" John asked.

"To produce all this wool?" Zack laughed, gesturing from wall to wall and into the other room. "You must be richer than my parents!"

John laughed. "I wouldn't say that."

"What's that box?" Ella asked, pointing to the flat-screen mounted on the wall.

"That's our TV," John said. He picked up the remote from the coffee table and pushed a button. The TV winked to life in the middle of a loud car chase scene.

The Egyptian kids all flinched and recoiled. Zack yelped and rolled out of the way like the car was about to run him over. "What sorcery is this?" he screamed.

John muted the volume and walked to block the screen, putting his hands up, palms out, gesturing that nothing was wrong. "It's okay! It's just pretend. It's fake. See?" He moved aside again.

"That looks pretty real to me!" Rich exclaimed. "What kind of chariots are those? Where are the horses?"

"Those are cars," John said. "They have engines inside that turn the wheels."

Zack, Rich, and Ella looked at John like he was speaking a foreign language.

"This future is very strange," Ella said, probably speaking for Zack and Rich as well.

John turned off the TV.

"And you can just wish it away, and away it goes," Zack said, in awe. "I like it here." He went over to a lamp on the end table and pulled on the chain dangling from the bulb. The light went out. He yanked on the chain again, and the bulb illuminated.

"Amazing," Zack said. "Must be some kind of flint-activated lever inside to start the fire in that little tube. Am I right? How does it work?"

John opened his mouth to teach Zack about filaments and Thomas Edison and electricity, but it seemed like too much to explain. Every invention built on something else before it. Going all the way back to the origin of those ideas seemed like such an overly complicated conversation. He didn't quite know where to begin that would make sense to Zack. Even if he started at the beginning (and what really was the beginning?), did John truly understand how electricity worked? Sure, he could repeat what he'd learned in school, but did he actually understand how a flow of electrons produced energy? And how could he explain an electron? Or an atom? He'd never personally seen an atom. He simply trusted the textbooks, that they truthfully represented human knowledge. It required a little imagination. And at some level, the textbooks were nothing more than stories passed down from one generation to the next. Scientific results that could be reproduced, sure, but if you got right down to it: What differentiated the particles that produced electrical energy from . . . magic?

After what John had experienced with his travels to ancient Egypt, who could say that Ra's light traveling across space and time wasn't in the same class of magic as electricity? And if electricity could be reproduced, could the magic of Ra be reproduced too? Could Ra's power be captured? Could John create a time-traveling device? The questions made him dizzy.

"John?" Zack said, stirring John from his spinning thoughts. "I asked how this lamp works—without oil?"

"It's—it's pretty much magic."

Zack smiled. "We say that about things we don't understand too. Or we attribute them to a god or goddess."

"I guess you could call these gods Volt and

Watt," John said.

Sarah walked back into the room and gave a thumbs-up. Good, everything was set with Maxine.

"Volt," Rich repeated. "Sounds like a powerful god."

"Definitely," Sarah said. "Electricity pretty much runs the world. Powers our TVs, our lights, our phones, our computers. Everything."

"The god of everything?" Ella said. "We don't really have one god for that."

"Well, not *everything*," John said. "There are things that can't be explained by electricity."

"Like how they stuffed those chariots into that little box on the wall?" Ella asked.

John chuckled. "Well, actually, those are beamed through wires into our house and interpreted by the software in our television. Pretty wild, if you think about it."

"Yeah," Sarah said, "we don't usually think about it."

John laughed.

"You're so lucky. You have a knob you turn to get the river flowing directly into your house,"

Rich said.

"You mean the sink?" John asked.

"Yeah, wonderful invention. We reroute the river to irrigate crops, but never all the way up to each house. Amazing."

"Our lives are definitely full of conveniences, that's for sure," Sarah said.

Mom came into the living room and asked Ella how she was feeling.

"Fine, thank you," Ella said. "I think the ice has turned back into water, though." She held the melted ice pack up in the air.

Mom took it and said, "I should give your parents a call. I hope they're not worried. You have that number, Sarah?"

"Yep!" Sarah pulled out her phone and texted her mom the number for Maxine. "That's their mom. Give her a try."

"Great. Thanks." Mom tapped the number and held the phone to her ear, walking out of the room. A moment later, they heard her talking to someone on the other end of the line.

John smiled. "Hope this works."

"Shh," Sarah said. "It will."

Rich shrugged at Sarah. "Who's she talking to?"

"It's your mom, silly," Sarah said, winking at Rich. "Don't worry, we've got it covered."

"You two are sneaky," Zack said, grinning. He butted shoulders with Sarah.

Mom came back to the doorway. "All set. Your mother sounded very nice. We didn't talk long because she was out to dinner with your dad. Date night."

"Can they stay over?" Sarah asked. John could tell she knew the answer.

"Yep!" Mom said.

All the kids gave a whoop of excitement, except Rich.

"I'll pull some new toothbrushes out," Sarah said. "And they can borrow some of our pajamas."

"Perfect," Mom said. "But before you brush, ice cream sundaes are ready in the kitchen."

"Yay!" John jumped up. "I call dibs on the chocolate sauce!"

"I don't know what that is," Zack said. "But I want some."

The next morning, John woke to the smell of pancakes cooking in butter on the griddle. If they were Dad's, they'd have sprinkles. If they were Mom's, they'd be pumpkin. Either way was a win.

He nudged Rich and Zack awake. They both barely roused, their hair pointing in every direction, their sleeping bags flopped open, their pajamas twisted on their bodies.

"You guys sleep all right?" John asked.

Rich only grunted in reply.

"I slept terrible," Zack said. "It's so noisy here."

"What d'you mean?" John said. He pushed his ear out to listen.

"Like that," Zack said, pointing toward the wall. "What's that roar?"

A car drove by outside.

"Or that," Zack added, pointing toward the ceiling.

Suddenly the sound of a distant propeller airplane overhead materialized to John. He chuffed. Only a second before, he hadn't even heard it. Then when Zack pointed it out, he realized it was there. It had been the same with the car.

"Just used to it, I guess," John said. "There's a small airport over that direction. Surprised you could even hear that."

"What's an airport?" Zack said, plugging his ears. "And why are they so noisy?"

Again, John watched his thoughts trip over themselves as he tried to figure out a way to explain something to Zack. Communicating what an airport is requires explaining airplanes. And explaining airplanes requires explaining the aerodynamics of flight, something that the Wright brothers wouldn't prove until more than four and a half thousand years after the time of Zack's life. And, really, did John understand how an airplane flies enough to convincingly teach someone?

A steel tube floats in the air on invisible currents, like a fish gliding through a stream.

Okay, there, silly. Magic.

"Let's just get some pancakes," John said instead, tossing his hand dismissively. "Do you like maple syrup?"

"Pancakes, yes. Maple syrup? I don't know what that is," Zack said. "But if it's at all like chocolate sauce, I'll have double."

John laughed.

"Actually," Zack said, "can I have chocolate sauce on my maple syrup?"

"That might be a little much . . ." John put his finger to his chin. "Or, you might be onto something delicious. Let's try it!"

Zack wriggled out of his sleeping bag and straightened his loaner Harry Potter pajamas. "You coming, Rich?"

Rich pulled the sleeping bag over his head and mumbled through the cotton, "—wanna go home."

"We will, we will," Zack said. "But there's time for more chocolate sauce first."

"And maple syrup," John added, smiling.

"Let's do it," Zack said.

John and Zack headed into the kitchen. Sarah and Ella sat on stools at the countertop, watching Mom at the griddle. Mom flipped a golden brown pancake with a hint of orange.

"Pumpkin it is," John said.

"I don't know what that is," Zack said.

"But you want some," John finished for him. "I got it." They both laughed.

"You know me so well!" Zack patted John on the back.

"Always ready to try new things, right, Zack?" Sarah added. "Me too. Although with that trip we took to, uh, your house, I think I could dial back the adventure for a little while."

"Hopefully not for too long, though," Mom said. "We move in a few days. That'll be a big adventure." She gestured around the kitchen with the spatula. Cardboard boxes stood open, most of the dishes packed, art removed from the walls.

This house didn't feel quite as much like a home anymore. Take all of their personal touches away and it looked more like an empty picture frame. Surveying the scene, John found that he wasn't feeling as attached to this place as he had before their journey to Egypt.

"It's just a house," John said. "We have a new one in Maryland."

Mom smiled and pulled John into her hip for a sideways hug. "That's right, sweetie. We'll turn it into our new home."

John scrunched his brow. He realized he didn't feel worried about the move. And that felt . . .

well, it felt odd not to feel worried. But he liked the airy feeling of it. He smiled.

"What's on your mind?" Mom asked.

"Nothing," John said. "Hungry for some pancakes."

"Good timing," Mom said, dishing the golden cakes onto plates in front of Sarah and Ella.

John grabbed a plate off the stack next to the stove. He saw Zack bent over, transfixed with the flame underneath the griddle.

"What do you burn?" Zack asked. He reached down and opened the cupboard underneath the stove and peered inside. "How do you keep the flame so consistent—but, where's the fuel?"

"Still going on with your theater production, eh?" Mom asked, looking to Sarah and rolling her eyes slightly.

"It's gas," John answered. "Natural gas." As he said it, the term seemed funny to him. Was there an unnatural gas?

"Gas," Zack repeated. "Don't know what that is, but—well, you know the rest. I tell ya. You guys have it all. You flick a switch, you get light. You push a button, chariots whiz into a box in your living room. You pull a handle, water. But I think the best one, probably my favorite so far, you turn this little knob and—poof—fire."

"You must have so much free time," Ella said, one cheek full of pancake and a drop of syrup hanging onto her lip. "You don't have to fetch water, start the fire, all the chores kids like us do back home." She picked up a link of sausage and chewed into one end.

"Oh, I want some of that," Zack said, reaching for a piece of sausage. He bit into it and froze. His eyes slowly widened, then his jaw moved again like a cow slowly chewing its cud. Then his eyes closed and he chewed more quickly. "I've never . . . tasted anything . . . so good."

"Just wait 'til you try it with syrup," John said, passing the bottle of Maine maple goodness.

Zack put the link down on a plate and poured the golden sugar onto it. "It looks like honey. We have that. It's sweet and yummy. And it stores well. We put it with our kings inside the pyramid so they have it in the afterlife."

John heard Mom chuckle.

"Well," Mom said, "it's been great getting to

know you kids. I texted your Mom this morning and let her know that she could come pick you up after breakfast. I hate to run you out, but we have more packing to do."

The loud clatter of a fork dropped onto a plate. Sarah looked up at John. "We can walk them home, Mom. It's fine."

"That's nice of you, but I'd like to meet their mom. Tell her what wonderful children she has." Mom gave a big toothy grin to Ella and Zack. "Where's Rich?"

"Here," Rich mumbled from the doorway.

Mom startled, throwing her hand to her chest. "Oh, didn't see you there. Come eat some breakfast."

Rich shuffled over, his eyes at half-mast.

"Did you sleep all right?" Mom asked.

"No." Rich took a plate and let Mom serve him a pancake. He sat down and started eating.

"Here," Ella said, handing the glass bottle of syrup to Rich. "Try this. It's delicious. Kinda like honey, but different."

"I don't want it," Rich said, shoving a bite into his mouth.

A silence fell over the kitchen. Mom flipped another pancake. Zack moaned with delight at the sausage dipped in syrup. Ella continued to eat but kept glancing over at Rich.

"Mom, can we pretty please walk them home?" Sarah asked. "We'll be fast. Promise."

Mom tilted her head to the side and stared at Sarah.

"We'll finish packing as soon as we get home," John added, hoping to tip the scales.

Dad walked in at that moment, scratching his head. "Good morning, whippersnappers. Who's ready for a big day?"

Zack chuckled and looked over to the other kids. No doubt he was reminded of his own father, Imhotep, who every night said that the next day would be a big one. Zack looked down at his empty plate. He pushed his fork around in the syrup, set it down, and stood. "I guess we probably should be going." He said it with sadness in his voice.

Rich straightened his back and put his fork down too. There were still a few bites left on his plate.

"I hate to leave," Ella said. "But I know we have to go home." She looked at John. "I don't think we could stay here as long as you stayed with us." She looked at Sarah. "I don't know how you kept it together for so long."

Sarah tousled her brother's hair. "We had each other to lean on."

John pushed her arm away and ran his hands through his hair to straighten it.

"Geez, did I ruin the party?" Dad said. "Or do I smell?" He put his nose to his armpit and took a big whiff, then recoiled and staggered back into the wall so hard it shook the plaster. He gagged and rolled his eyes back until all that could be seen were the whites. Slumping to the floor, he made a few choking noises, twitched his body once, twice, and finally exhaled a last breath, his tongue hanging out of his mouth.

"Bravo!" Mom clapped her hands. "We definitely have a house full of actors around here."

Dad jumped to his feet, a broad grin on his face, then took a bow.

John chuckled. Sarah laughed too, but with an accompanying roll of the eyes. While the Tidewells laughed together, John noticed that Zack wasn't smiling. He was just staring at them. Same with Ella. And Rich.

While John had shared a silly and lighthearted moment with his family, he could tell the Egyptian kids were thinking about their own families. John was reminded of how he felt when playing the Senet game with Zack and Imhotep and Hatmehit. It had been fun, and comforting, but that same joy had also served as a reminder of what he was missing.

"Mom," John whispered to get her attention without a big fuss. "Have you heard back from their mom?"

She pulled her phone from a pocket in her robe. "Nope, not yet. Why?" She leaned closer to John to make it easier for him to whisper in her ear.

"I think they miss home. Can we just walk them? Please? Maybe their parents aren't even awake yet. Date night and all."

Mom chuckled. "We Tidewells are early risers." She glanced at Rich, who still looked like he could fall back asleep any second if he were only to lie down. "Okay, I guess that's all right. You're sweet to think of their feelings in that way, Johnny. Love you." She pecked at his forehead.

John pumped his fist in victory. "Yes!"

"What?" Sarah asked.

"Mom said we can walk Zack and Rich and Ella home."

Sarah smiled to Ella, who smiled to Zack, who smiled to Rich. All eyes went to Rich's straight face. After a couple of quiet seconds, the corner of Rich's mouth crooked upward and then stretched across his lips. His cheeks tugged against his eyes, his smile bright for all to see.

"Let's go!" Rich said. "Thank you for the pancakes, Mrs. Tidewell."

"You're quite welcome, Rich. Why don't you go change out of those pajamas. They're pretty tight on you." Mom pointed to Rich's bicep, the shirt stretched against his arm. When Rich stood from his stool, a thin line of his stomach was visible. The pant legs came up to mid-shin.

The kids all giggled and Rich joined them. He seemed happy now that he knew they were heading home.

After the Egyptian kids had changed back into

their "*costumes*," as Dad put it, they said goodbye to Mr. and Mrs. Tidewell and headed out the back door.

Crossing the backyard toward the gate that led up into the mountains, John heard his dad's voice.

"Where are you going?"

"Taking Zack and Rich and Ella home," John said, his tone impatient because it was obvious what they'd just discussed. His dad crossed his arms.

Oh, but why were they headed out the back gate and into the mountains when all the houses were out the front door and on the road? John thought quickly on his feet. "Sorry, Dad. Yeah, uh, there's a shortcut over here. It's faster."

Dad cocked his head. "I don't know of any shortcuts or houses in that direction. You know you're to go straight to their house, then directly back here. Understood?"

John thought of traveling back to ancient Egypt, and shivered. "Understood. Don't worry. We'll be back soon."

Dad waved him off and headed back inside.

"Nice thinking there, bro," Sarah said as they

hiked up the hill.

When they got to the switchback near the cave, Sarah went first.

"Careful here," John said. "I slipped and rolled down this hill the first time I went through here."

"Yeah, me too," Ella said, pointing to her bandaged ankle. Fortunately, the swelling had gone down and she was walking fine on it.

"Oh, right," John said, smiling. "Still, wanna take my hand?"

Ella kept her eyes on John's, but her chin tucked down slightly. Was the pink in her cheeks getting darker?

She extended her hand and John took it. It felt warm and soft and he liked it.

"Too bad we can't play together more," John said as he and Ella traversed the narrow off-trail path to the cave entrance.

"Maybe you could visit again someday!" Ella said, excited about the idea.

John tilted his head side to side. "Maybe." The idea of traveling to ancient Egypt ever again sounded daunting, but now that they knew how it worked—tracing the eye of Ra—and which passage, specifically, the idea of *not* ever going back seemed absurd. It was such a great opportunity for learning. Just think of what more they could discover.

At the cave entrance, Ella squeezed John's hand, then let go. John put his arms around her and she hugged him back. They held it for a moment and when he pulled away, Ella had a tear on the edge of her eye.

"Here," Zack said. Hanging from his fist was the necklace, the leather strap holding the jade pendant of the eye of Ra. "I want you two to keep this. To remember us."

"We could never forget you," Sarah said. She accepted the gift into her palms as if it were a sacred token.

John unlatched his wristwatch and held it out. "It'll freeze when you go through," he said. "But I want you to have it. So you can remember us too."

"This has been like a dream," Zack said. "And *unlike* a dream. Dreams fade when you wake, but I have a feeling this memory will be with us always. Forever."

"Thanks for helping us," Sarah said. "Not sure

what we would have done if we hadn't met you." Her eyelashes blinked and she smiled a coy grin. Then she pulled Zack in for a hug. He looked surprised, but pleased, and hugged her back.

Sarah let go and moved aside so John could say goodbye too.

"Respect," John said, thumping his chest twice, then giving a peace sign.

Zack chuckled. "That's good. Respect." He repeated the gesture, thumping on his own chest.

"Okay," Rich said. "Goodbye, then." His eyes caught Sarah's for the briefest moment, then he looked away.

Sarah dashed over and bear-hugged Rich, his arms pinned at his sides. "You're a good kid, Rich. Thanks for watching out for us. Respect." She pounded her chest twice and snorted some air from her nostrils.

The side of Rich's mouth turned up again in a half smile. "Thanks."

The Egyptian kids waved once more, then headed into the cave. The light from the morning sun shone directly in, but only so far. As the kids walked farther down, they seemed to dissipate into the dark, then they turned into the side passage with the hieroglyphs and disappeared from view.

A few moments passed. Then a few more.

"I wonder if they forgot how to do it," John said. "Or which one."

"No, I explained it carefully," Sarah said. She inhaled a quick burst. "I wonder if the magic stopped or it's used up or something. What if—"

A bright flash, more brilliant than the sunlight on their backs, burst from the cave, blinding them both and rendering them speechless.

Birds chirped in surprise. A distant plane lumbered overhead. John opened his eyes.

"Zack!" Sarah yelled. "Rich! Ella!"

There was no reply. The Egyptian kids were gone.

CHAPTER FIFTEEN

An Egyptian Returns

SARAH

Over the next several days, Sarah focused on packing up her room and helping out around the house. She'd only ever lived in this house for all of her life; she'd only ever known this bedroom. That meant she had a lot of stuff to filter through. As her dad said, moving was a great opportunity to simplify, to de-clutter, to reevaluate what you really need or use versus what you just have lying around.

There were two open boxes in Sarah's room at all times during her packing and assessing. One was marked "Thrift Store" and the other was marked "Sarah's Bedroom." She'd pull a toy from the back of her closet, and if she deemed it important enough to keep, she'd toss it in the box for her bedroom. If it was something she'd forgotten she even owned, or, as was the case more often, it was something she'd outgrown, then she'd toss it in the Thrift Store box. This wasn't always an easy decision.

"Whatcha doin'?" John asked, leaning on the doorjamb to Sarah's room.

Sarah sat on the floor with an old doll. It was missing one eye and its clothes were ragged, its face dirty and smeared with something dark— crayon? chocolate? mud?

"Not sure what to do with Binky," Sarah said, holding the doll up for John to see. "I never play with her anymore." As an aside, she looked directly at Binky. "Sorry, Binky." Then back to John, she said, "I'm having trouble just tossing her away forever. I mean, we've been through a lot together."

"When's the last time you even saw her?" John asked.

Sarah made a thoughtful face. "Don't know. Years, I guess."

"And in all that time, you still had her with you, right?" John said, fingering the eye of Ra pendant suspended around his neck.

Sarah smiled. "Yeah, I guess so. I won't ever forget her."

"Whether you keep that old nasty doll or not," John said.

"Hey," Sarah said, hugging Binky close with a frown on her face. "Don't call her nasty."

John cocked his head to the side in a questioning manner.

"Okay," Sarah said, getting a whiff of the musty old doll. It smelled like dried vomit. "She *is* pretty nasty." She tossed Binky toward the Thrift Store box.

Mom came around the corner as Binky arced through the air. "That's probably trash." She pointed to the large black trash bag hanging from Sarah's doorknob.

"She's not totally used up yet," Sarah said. "I bet she still has some love to give some little person out there."

Mom smiled. "If you think so, then it must be true. Your room is looking very clean. Almost done!"

"Thanks, Mom," Sarah said. Her eye caught John still fiddling with the necklace. "Hey, after we finish our rooms—"

"I'm already done," John said, beaming.

"After we finish our rooms," Sarah continued, "do you think it'd be okay if we go say goodbye to Zack and Rich and Ella one more time?"

John stopped twisting the necklace. He didn't smile like Sarah was hoping to see. They hadn't discussed another visit after they watched the Egyptian kids disappear into the cave a few days ago, but the notion that they could travel back through time had gnawed at Sarah ever since. Shouldn't they try to go back? At first, she'd felt entirely reluctant to leave her family again, but after stewing on it for a few days, thinking about how easily they'd returned once they knew the secret way to initiate the portal, and how easily Zack and Rich and Ella had done the same—it seemed no more challenging than getting on an airplane and trusting it to take you where you want to go. The first time you ride, you don't know what to expect and every jostle or sound is cause for excitement and alarm. But then you get used to it and it's easy. What could be easier than simply tracing a hieroglyph?

John didn't look like he wanted to experience that travel again, though.

"That'd be fine with me," Mom said. "Tell them hi for me and if they're ever in Maryland, they should come visit." She smiled and kept walking down the hall with a box in her arms.

"John?" Sarah said.

John walked into her room and sat down cross-legged on the floor.

"I don't know," John said, finally.

"Come on," Sarah nudged. "Mom and Dad won't even miss us. Remember how time froze here while we were gone? I mean, we could go to ancient Egypt for a month and come back at the same time we left. That's pretty amazing."

"It's awesome," John said. "Maybe we should tell someone at the museum. They'd love a chance like this."

"I've thought about that too," Sarah said. "Of

course, they'd think we're being silly. But, we should probably try."

"We tell Mom and Dad first?" John asked. "Then we go to the museum?"

"There's something else . . ." Sarah let the words hang out there.

"What?" John asked.

"Think about this: What would happen if word got out about this time-traveling space portal? I mean, wouldn't everyone want to try it? What if there is suddenly a big line of traffic and thousands of people are going back to ancient Egypt. Imagine whoever owns that land wants to sell tickets and T-shirts and souvenirs. Does the government get involved? And what happens in Zack's time? People littering and taking pictures and climbing on the pyramid and who knows what else. It could cause some kind of cross-time contamination. I mean, who knows if we already caused problems by going back there the first time?"

"Whoa," John said, holding his hands up. "I think you've watched too many *Twilight Zone* episodes."

"But seriously," Sarah said. "If someone from our time goes to ancient Egypt and teaches them about electricity, let's say, that would dramatically alter their—their everything. I don't know—their expectations of the world. Would they develop it, to use electrical power? And what would that mean for our time? Would our technology be more advanced than it is now?"

"Hey, that could be interesting to find out," John said, his finger on his chin.

"But we can't play like a god to them. That'd be dangerous. I mean, what if we—what if something like that changed history so much that we weren't even born? Would we come back to this time but cease to exist? Or be trapped in ancient Egypt? I can't even wrap my mind around it all."

John opened and closed his mouth several times like a guppy. "I—I don't know what to say."

"I think," Sarah said definitively, "we should go back once more and say goodbye to Zack and Rich and Ella. Forever. We should tell them that we're going to destroy the hieroglyph of the eye of Ra so that the portal can't ever be used again."

"So we don't end up destroying the world or

something," John said.

Sarah chuckled, but in a *yeah, seriously* kind of way.

"You realize what this means if we carry out your plan?" John asked.

Sarah shrugged. It meant a thousand things!

"We'd be sabotaging the pyramid of Djoser," John said. "We'd be the saboteurs."

"Well, besides Aten, you mean," Sarah said. "We saw him cut off the head of Serket."

"But if Aten knew about the portal, couldn't he be altering history too?" John asked.

"Shoot," Sarah said. "I hadn't thought of that."

"All the more reason to destroy the portal," John said.

"Before he does any real harm," Sarah agreed. "Okay, let's go."

She stood and headed for the door.

"But Mom said we could only go once you were done packing," John said, gesturing to the last pile of toys Sarah had left to process.

"I think those can wait. Saving the universe is probably more important." Sarah walked out her bedroom door.

"Save the universe?" John mumbled, then turned and ran after his sister.

Sarah wiped at the sweat dripping into her eyes. She kept pushing uphill, her leg muscles burning with the speed. About twenty yards behind, John struggled to keep up. She wouldn't let him get out of her sight, but the urgency to get to the cave, to alert Zack and Rich and Ella, and to shut down the portal—she felt like if she didn't hurry, something very, very bad could happen.

At the switchback where they'd headed off trail, she stood facing downhill, watching and waiting for John to catch up. "Hurry!"

John neared, breathing heavy and unable to speak. He slicked his brow with his forearm and looked up at her, then over to the cave's entrance behind Sarah.

Suddenly John's face paled. He couldn't speak, but his arm shot up, his finger pointing toward the cave. John dropped down onto his stomach.

Sarah whipped her head around toward the

cave. At the entrance stood an old man with gray hair and a gray beard, dressed in a full-length Egyptian robe. At his feet sat a full sack. It appeared that he hadn't seen Sarah or John, but Sarah did the same thing as John: she dropped to the ground, then scrambled behind a boulder, hidden from the mystery man's view.

"Who is it?" John whispered, still mostly out of breath.

"I don't know, but the robe . . ." Something about that robe lingered in Sarah's mind.

John peeked over the edge of the boulder. Sarah followed.

The old man leaned against one side of the cave. He had his eyes closed and he held his face up to the sky, soaking up the sunlight. He took a deep breath in through his nostrils, then exhaled through his mouth.

"I remember," Sarah whispered, then ducked back down behind the boulder, pulling John down too. "The old man who was talking with Hatmehit under the structure that day. When we told Imhotep about Aten."

John's eyes squinted and he looked up and to

the left, searching his memories for that moment. "Oh, I think I remember. Maybe."

"What's he doing here?" Sarah asked.

"Only one way to find out," John said. He stood from behind the boulder.

"Wait!" Sarah hissed, pulling on John's shirt.

But it was too late. The man heard them and opened his eyes. When he turned to look at the kids, Sarah knew immediately who he was. It wasn't who she'd thought.

The man staring at them had distinct, bright green eyes.

"It can't be," Sarah said. "Aten?"

The man grinned, then bent over with his arms out like he was balancing himself for a springing action. Was he going to come after and attack them? Or bolt back into the cave?

Then he noticed John and straightened his posture a little.

"You?" Aten said in surprise, looking directly at John. "You exposed me to Imhotep. It's your fault I had to flee from Saqqara."

"I didn't force you to steal from the pyramid," John said, defiant. He balled his fists.

"Aten, what are you doing here?" Sarah asked. "And what happened to you? You look so—old."

"If you're here in this time—" Aten said. "That must mean you know about the portal of Ra's light. I knew it! That's why you called them police instead of guards back in my time. That was nagging at me."

"Aten," Sarah said. "Why are you so old now?"

"From using the portal. It ages you. When you returned to this time, though only a second or two may have passed for the people here, you are older than when you saw them last."

Sarah flashed back to her dad commenting that they looked older when they'd first returned. She'd chalked it up to typical sentimental dad stuff, but maybe it was from the portal—it had aged them. Looking at Aten, he had aged a lifetime—

"But you're an old man," John said.

"I've traveled many times through the portal," Aten said, tugging on his beard. "It has been profitable. And tiring." He chuckled to himself and sighed.

"The artifacts from the pyramid," Sarah said.

"Why'd you steal them?"

Aten exhaled a longer sigh and bowed his chin to his chest. "I'm not proud of that. I stumbled across the portal and it brought me to this world—your era—and I loved it." He looked up with a gleam in his eye and a sad smile pulling his lips tight. "I sold my necklace to a collector of Egyptian relics and lived on that money for a while. I became greedy for all the conveniences. I wanted to live here forever. But when I ran out of money, I became a beggar and was forced to travel home to Egypt using the portal. I tried to go back to my normal life there—working on the pyramid, helping Imhotep—but I couldn't get this place out of my mind. I knew I needed money to return and so I—I resorted to burglary. I know it wasn't right. I'm sorry. I'm so sorry." He hung his head and a tear fell to the earth.

John and Sarah stood speechless. Another tear fell silently from Aten's cheek.

John took a few steps toward Aten. Sarah watched him go but didn't make any move to stop him.

A sudden loud clatter of rocks above made them

look upslope. An elk bounced up the scree, knocking rocks loose with each bound of its massive bulk. The stones tumbled down toward them. Sarah yanked John by the shoulders out of the way of a rock the size of a cannonball.

Aten shouted a fearful shriek that made Sarah's hair stand on end. John's shoulders shivered beneath her grasp.

Aten put his arms up, but nothing could save him. A massive boulder had slipped loose from its mooring in the hillside as easily as a grain of sand rolling down a dune. The earth itself seemed to shift and slump in one enormous glide of rock and dirt and sediment. A rock slide pummeled down and around the cave entrance, enveloping Aten along with it.

Sarah looked away.

A cloud of dust billowed toward Sarah and John. They automatically ducked and shielded themselves from the dirt-laden wind. Sarah was reminded of the sandstorm.

When the dust cleared, they surveyed the damage.

The cave's entrance had been demolished. To

the side, Aten lay half buried by rubble, a gash on his forehead with a ribbon of blood.

"Is he dead?" John said. He nudged Aten with a stick and jumped back, waiting for a response.

"John!" Sarah snapped. "You don't poke people with a stick. Especially if they're dead, sheesh!"

"If they're dead, what do they care?" John said.

"What about respect?"

Aten moaned, frightening Sarah enough that she lurched sideways. John crouched with the stick raised like a sword.

"He's alive!" John said. "What do we do?"

Sarah pulled out her phone. "I'm calling the police."

"Call Mom and Dad," John said.

"I'll call them next."

Aten had one hand free, but his other was pinned under the debris. He moved his arm to his head and moaned again. "Wha—happen?" He blinked his glassy green eyes.

For a fleeting moment, Sarah felt bad for him. Then she wondered how they were going to explain all this to the police.

And to their parents.

"You did the right thing by calling us," Officer Wilhelm said. His bushy mustache bounced when he talked, and it was all Sarah could do not to watch it ripple up and down like a dancing caterpillar.

"Thank you, Officer," Sarah said. "We were just coming home from saying goodbye to our friends and found him like this, unconscious. It was pretty freaky."

"Yes, thank you, Officer," Mom said, pulling Sarah close.

John stood nearby with Dad's arm around his shoulders.

"We've been looking for this guy." The officer gestured to Aten lying on a stretcher, moaning, two EMTs securing him in place, another police officer keeping watch. "Been calling him the Egyptian Enigma."

"What's an enigma?" John asked.

"An enigma is a puzzle, a riddle, something perplexing," Officer Wilhelm said, the caterpillar on his upper lip doing a break-dance move. "This guy has befuddled us. He appears out of nowhere and sells some pristine ancient Egyptian artifact on the black market. We have no inkling of where he gets the treasures or how he transports them. It's like he conjures them out of thin air . . ." The officer shook his head, scratching the back of his neck as if it would help massage his mind into solving the riddle. "Then he disappears again. Vanishes without a trace like he never existed. Until sometime later he turns up again with another valuable artifact. It doesn't make sense."

"It definitely doesn't make sense," John agreed. He thought about trying to explain electricity or cars or airplanes to Zack. How could he explain a magic portal to the policeman?

"Huh?" Officer Wilhelm pushed up his cap.

"Nothing," John said. "Maybe he was hiding in these mountains."

"You said there was a cave up here. Maybe he was using it to hide his loot," Dad said.

"Geez," Mom said. "You're lucky you found him trapped in this landslide. He's a dangerous man. Who knows what could have happened?"

"I don't think he was dangerous," Sarah said. "Just a man without a home." She glanced side-long to John. He was looking toward the cave with a frown.

The cave entrance had been buried by tons of rock. Had it collapsed the secret passage, destroyed the eye of Ra?

Guess that's what we came here to do anyway, Sarah told herself. Even so, she had hoped to say good-bye one more time to Zack and Rich and Ella. But maybe it was better this way. She wasn't meant to be in ancient Egypt any more than Zack and Rich and Ella—or Aten!—were meant to be here. It wasn't natural, and Mother Nature prevented anyone from using the portal ever again.

CHAPTER SIXTEEN

Maryland

JOHN

A month later, John sat on the bed in his new bed-room in Maryland, several boxes still unpacked, only a handful of his Denver Nuggets posters on the walls. He tossed a fist-size squishy basketball into the small hoop on the back of his door.

"Swish!" he called out loud, and looked down to the iPad propped on his desk. Roman's face cheered back via FaceTime.

"Oh, that was a beauty!" Roman said. "Okay, my turn."

John watched as Roman, almost 1,700 miles

away back in Colorado, arced a similar squishy ball through the air at a similar hoop on the back of his own bedroom door. The two hoops had been a moving present from Roman. One for John, one for Roman.

"Oh, brick. Dang," Roman said, swiping his fist through the air in defeat.

"That makes it nineteen to eighteen, my lead," John said. "But it's first to twenty-one, so you could still win it with a three-pointer if I miss this one."

John rolled his neck, then waved his arms back and forth like he saw the pros do, stretching his shoulders. "No pressure, no pressure. Okay, I got this."

Roman drummed his palms on his thighs to make a rumbling sound, his voice mimicking a raucous cheering crowd of thousands.

John took aim, felt the ball light on his palm, then pushed it into the air and watched it fly like a graceful bird on course to its nest. John could feel another swish about to happen, and he tensed his body, willing it to be so.

Suddenly the door swung open, batting the ball

into the desk, knocking the iPad off its perch and onto the floor.

Roman moaned as if he'd actually fallen. "Ow. What was that?"

"No! Interference," John yelled, pointing at Sarah standing in the doorway, twiddling a strand of her red hair.

Sarah didn't even seem to realize or care that she'd just interrupted his victory shot. "Turn on the radio."

John picked up the iPad, talking to Roman. "I get to take that shot over. Clearly interference."

"Agreed," Roman said.

"Turn on the radio!" Sarah shouted.

John flinched and looked over at her. "Sheesh, what's the big deal?"

"You'll hear—if you turn on the radio!"

"Roman, I gotta go," John said. "Let's continue this later, okay?"

"Oh man, this is a wild time for a commercial break, but that's how we roll. Later." Roman thumped his chest twice and flashed a peace sign, then stabbed his forefinger toward the screen and disappeared from view.

"NPR," Sarah said. "Hurry."

"Okay, okay," John said, looking at Sarah. "What's the big deal?"

John opened the NPR app on his iPad.

"Adam Williams here, talking with Egyptologist Sandra Ewing about her discovery yesterday in the Pyramid of King Djoser. This is a historically significant structure in that it was the first pyramid of its kind, designed by the architect Imhotep sometime in the twenty-seventh century BCE. What did you uncover, Professor Ewing?"

John lost his snarky attitude and realized he was holding his breath in anticipation of what had been found. He looked up at Sarah, who swallowed so hard he could see her throat bob up and down.

"The most amazing and mystifying discovery I've made in my forty-year career," said professor of Egyptology Sandra Ewing. *We can't explain it."*

"Describe it for our listeners."

"It's pretty straightforward to understand what the object actually is, since they're common in our time. But wristwatches weren't common in ancient Egypt, which is why it's so unexplainable to us. A wristwatch

is not something ever uncovered from this epoch."

"And it's not some sort of hoax or prank?"

"That would certainly make it easier to dismiss. But we've used radiocarbon dating to confirm that this particular timepiece was in fact buried in the pyramid with King Djoser nearly five thousand years ago. Simply astounding."

John's jaw dropped at the same time his eyebrows went up, as if both jaw and eyebrows were on the same hinge pulling them from the back. His skin tingled and he could feel his arm hairs spike to attention.

"Yeah," Sarah said, nodding slowly.

"The watch was embedded in a wall of stone upon which were a set of hieroglyphs that we've never seen before."

"You're saying there is a section of the pyramid that has yet been undiscovered until now? How could something like this elude researchers in such a well-studied pyramid?"

"Exactly, Adam. I'm a scientist and so I have no trouble admitting that we have no idea as to what's going on here."

"There were no other clues at all? What did the new-

ly discovered hieroglyphs tell you?"

"They seem to be a children's fable. Or maybe a tale of King Djoser as a child with a goddess, probably fabricated to make him look superhuman and justify his kingship."

"Would you mind telling us some of what they showed?"

"Of course. The carvings depict a boy with a dimple only on his right cheek—the symbolism of which is unclear—and a girl with fiery hair. We're still analyzing, but we think maybe the boy is meant to be King Djoser and we haven't yet placed what goddess the fire-headed child could be. The first set of glyphs describes a confrontation with a cobra, where the boy stares it down until it starts dancing. The snake charmer mythos is relatively common, but rarely does the charmer use his eyes. Again, building up the king to be a divine being capable of superhuman feats."

John blurted out a laugh. He certainly hadn't felt superhuman when he was eye to eye with that cobra. Sarah sniggered and put her hand to her mouth. And besides, Zack was the one who had made the cobra dance, by waving the necklace's pendant.

"The next frame describes the boy jumping over a vast sea of scorpions inside a confined space, the fiery-haired girl trapped on the other side. Here, we think, it shows that he saved the goddess at one point."

"Yeah, right!" Sarah puffed, rolling her eyes so hard that her head went with it.

"And the last frame is the most interesting, in my opinion. I think we'll be studying them for years to come, but the last is the most revealing about their relationship. It shows the boy swimming away from a crocodile in water. We think that could be the Nile River, since crocodiles are common there. The interesting bit is that as the boy nears the shore, the fire-haired goddess pulls him out of the water onto the sand. The final frame is them resting together, staring up at Ra. The light of Ra then seems to carry them, like a ferry across the river, toward the stars."

"Fascinating," the commentator said. Then, rare for live radio, there was an extended moment of silence, long enough for John to look at his iPad, wondering if it had shut down.

"Fascinating," Adam Williams said again.

The professor piped in, *"I couldn't agree more."*

"Well, next up," Adam continued, *"we have anoth-*

er visiting professor to weigh in on—"

John closed the NPR app. It was fortunate he was standing near his bed because it caught him when his legs gave out and he flopped down onto it.

He held out his arm to show Sarah his shaking hand.

"We changed history, John. I also researched Imhotep and Hatmehit," Sarah said. "I was starting to wonder if it was all some sort of dream or hallucination."

"I know what you mean," John said, his eyes staring at the hardwood floor. "I keep thinking about Zack's final words, how he thought this was unlike a dream, that it wouldn't fade." Then he looked up at his sister. "But it kind of *is* fading, isn't it?"

Sarah hesitated, then gave one slight nod of agreement. "But I don't want it to."

"Me neither," John said. "I think it's because we haven't been talking about it."

Sarah sat next to John on the bed. "So, let's talk about it."

For the next hour, they told each other every

detail they could recall about the trip to ancient Egypt. The highs, the lows, the close calls, the laughs, the happiness, the sadness—they reveled in it all as one big gift.

A subtle knock on the door interrupted them as John was recounting the taste of the tilapia barley stew.

"Come in," John said.

Dad pushed open the door. "Whatcha doin'?"

"Remembering Zack and Rich and Ella." Sarah smiled.

"Oh, that's nice," Dad said. He tucked his hands in his pockets and leaned against the doorjamb. "Mind if I listen in?"

"Did you know Hatmehit was the goddess of fish in ancient Egypt?" Sarah said.

John laughed. "Really?"

Sarah nodded. "According to Wikipedia. I mean, that was a pretty good fish stew she made."

"Well, take it from a fire-haired goddess to know," John said, poking his sister in the side.

Sarah giggled and tickled him back.

"Yo," Dad interrupted. "I'm trying to think of something for dinner. Any ideas?"

John escaped his sister's sneaky fingernails and regained his breath. "Tilapia barley stew?"

"Yeah!" Sarah exclaimed.

"Tilapia?" Dad looked at them. "Who are you children? And what have you done with my kids?"

"I'll make it," John volunteered.

Dad put both hands over his heart and staggered on his feet, pretending to die yet again. "Be still my beating heart. My boy is making dinner again."

"Funny, Dad," John sneered. "I'll make a list for the store. There's one ingredient we probably won't have: water from the Nile drawn at sunset. But the rest we can get easy enough."

"Water from the Nile at sunset," Dad echoed. "Dramatic. I like it. You should be a writer, Johnny." He wagged his finger at John.

"Don't forget the garlic," Sarah said.

"Of course," John said. "Added at just the right time. Not too early—"

Both John and Sarah finished it together: "And not too late."

Dad laughed and shook his head. "You kids

constantly surprise me. I love it."

"You don't know the half of it, Dad."

"Ha! I'm sure I don't," Dad said. "But let's keep some mystery, okay?"

"So, can I drive to the store?" Sarah asked.

Dad popped a loud laugh. "Really getting ahead of yourself there, aren't you, sweetie?"

"I'm probably a little older than you think I am."

John chuckled.

"I'll drive this time," John said.

They all laughed together.

EPILOGUE

Winter had descended on Colorado and that meant the mountain slopes were coated with snow. A fresh powder had fallen overnight and two siblings—Casey and Lisa—were taking advantage of the mountain out their backyard gate. With skis lashed to their packs, they hiked up the hill, intent on making the trip down much faster than the way up. Their breath puffed out like a dragon's in the cold air.

"Smells good out here," Casey said.

Lisa nodded. "I love it. I'm glad Mom moved to Colorado."

"Should we race down the hill?" Casey asked, as he always did.

"Don't we always?" Lisa replied.

"Let's go through the trees this time, make it

more interesting." Casey rubbed his gloved hands together and they crinkled in the cold.

"Sure," Lisa said. "How about last one to the bottom has to do the winner's laundry for a month?"

"Oh, you're so on," Casey said, picking up his pace to the top.

They were fraternal twins, thirteen years old, and had moved into this new house with their mom only a few months earlier when the family that used to live there moved to Maryland.

"I think it was somewhere around here they caught that thief guy," Lisa said, nodding to a particularly steep part of the slope.

"The Egyptian Enigma," Casey said. "Yeah."

"What a kooky name. Why do the police always make up names for the bad guys?"

"I think the media make up the names," Casey said. "Gets more viewers if there's a story."

"Everyone loves a good story," Lisa said. She stopped and swung her pack around to the ground. Untying her skis, she set them parallel to each other on a small horizontal shelf of crusty snow in the downslope shade of a large evergreen tree.

Casey did the same.

"Okay," Lisa said, pulling her goggles down from her helmet and over her eyes. "Ready?"

"Ready," Casey said, nodding, making his helmet jiggle.

"Three . . . two . . . one . . . Go!"

As usual, Lisa's start beat Casey's, though he could usually catch her on the stretches. The wind whipped across their faces as they sliced through the trees.

Casey's ski slid on a surprise patch of icy snow and he faltered, letting Lisa take a strong lead. Casey jumped over into her tracks and used the worn path to increase his speed.

Suddenly Lisa disappeared.

One second she was right in front of Casey, the next she went straight down like a trapdoor had opened and swallowed her whole.

Casey threw his skis sideways and pushed a rooster tail of snow out to stop himself as quickly as possible.

"Lisa!" He used his poles to unclasp the bindings from his boots. "Lisa!"

Two steps downhill and he saw the gaping hole. At the bottom of a steep drop, Lisa lay flat on her back on a pile of powdery snow. Her body's imprint looked like one of those cartoons where the person runs through a wall and leaves the exact cutout of their body.

Lisa's eyes were wide open and she shook her head, spitting out snow.

"You okay?" Casey shouted. He looked for a way down and saw that, with the angle of the hill, he could probably walk into the hole from the front as if it were a cave's entrance.

"I'm all right," Lisa said, doubt in her voice. "I think. Surprisingly." She leaned forward. Both skis had come off with the impact, but they were on the dirt floor not far from her, unscathed.

"I'm coming down," Casey said, traversing the steep embankment to get to his sister.

Lisa fumbled in her pack for a flashlight. "Always prepared." She turned on the torch and lit the interior. Casey saw a tunnel, like staring into a dark throat of the yawning mountain.

"Whoa, cool," Lisa said. She stood and dusted herself off, then walked further into the passage.

Casey followed. "This place is kinda spooky," he said, glancing around.

A side passage cut to the right. Lisa took it, but after a few steps she said, "It's a dead end." She turned around, her flashlight strafing the wall.

"What was that?" Casey asked, pointing behind Lisa.

She turned back and illuminated the wall. Carvings in the stone danced with their shadows.

"Are those—hieroglyphs?" Casey asked.

"Like, from ancient Egypt?" Lisa shone the light closer to the strange markings.

"Did we find the cave where that Enigma guy was hiding his treasure?" Casey asked. "The police excavated around here for a while, but they never found the cave that those kids said was supposed to be here. Maybe this is it."

"Look," Lisa said, focusing her beam on one particular hieroglyph. "The eye of Ra. We studied this last year in World History. Ra was a powerful god to the ancient Egyptians. Rowed the sun barge across the sky every day."

Casey stared at the hieroglyph, studying it: the eye and brow, the line shooting diagonally with the curlicue finish, another line pointing straight down with a knife's edge. The carving seemed to speak to Casey in some strange and silent way. He wanted to hear what it was saying, so he moved a little closer.

"Casey," Lisa said, caution in her tone.

He suddenly felt an urge to reach out, to touch the carving, to feel it with his bare skin. Casey removed his glove and placed a finger gently into the groove of the eye, then traced around and down the diagonal line ending with the curlicue finish. His finger tingled as he looped around to the line with the knife's edge.

Tilapia Barley Stew

This is adapted from a real recipe used by the ancient Egyptians according to *Cooking in Ancient Civilizations* by Cathy K. Kaufman, with some liberties added.

- 1/2 cup barley (rinsed to remove surface starch)
- 3 cups water (from the Nile if you can swing it, but make sure to filter it first)
- 4 green onions, sliced
- 2 tilapia fillets, cut into bite-size chunks
- 2 cloves of garlic, minced
- salt to taste

Boil the barley in the water, then simmer for 30 minutes. Skim off any foam (starch) that rises to the surface. Add the tilapia. Cook for approximately 10 minutes on medium. Add the scallions and garlic and cook for 5 minutes. Add salt to taste. Enjoy like John and Sarah and the ancient Egyptians.

About the Author

Ben Gartner is the award-winning author of The Eye of Ra adventure series for middle graders. His books take readers for a thrilling ride, maybe even teaching them something in the meantime. Ben can be found living and writing near the mountains with his wife and two boys.

BenGartner.com
Twitter: @BGartnerWriting
Facebook: @BenGartnerAuthor
Instagram: @BGartnerWriting

Read the exciting series!

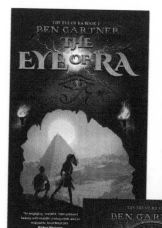
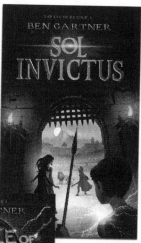

Made in the USA
Columbia, SC
01 August 2022

64402526R00167